THE WEIGHT OF GOODBYE

NOT ALL GOODBYES ARE THE END

UDIT TIWARI

"To my parents—
The silent warriors of my life, whose sacrifices went unnoticed by the world but never by me.
You have carried burdens I may never fully understand, yet you walked forward with unwavering love, shielding me from storms while weathering them yourselves.
This book is not just my dream—it is a reflection of your strength, your struggles, and the values you instilled in me.
For every lesson, every moment of patience, and every silent prayer whispered for my success—this is for you.
With all my heart, I thank you."

Contents

Contents

Foreword

Every story is a journey, not just for its characters but for the one who writes it. The Weight of Goodbye is more than just a tale of love, loss, and self-discovery and it is a piece of my heart, woven into words.

This book was born from a deep place of reflection, inspired by the struggles we all face when choosing between our ambitions and the bonds that tether us to home. Aarav's story is, in many ways, a reflection of the silent battles we fight within ourselves, the longing for something greater, the guilt of leaving behind what we love, and the aching question: Did I make the right choice?

At its core, this book is about the weight we carry when we say goodbye—not just to people, but to versions of ourselves, to dreams that shift, and to the places that shaped us. It is a story for anyone who has ever felt torn between duty and desire, between past and future.

I hope that as you turn these pages, you find a piece of your own journey within Aarav's. May his choices remind you that sometimes, goodbyes aren't endings; they are the bridges to new beginnings.

With gratitude,
UDIT TIWARI

Preface

Stories have a way of finding us when we need them the most. The Weight of Goodbye is one such story,one that came to me not just as a writer but as a person who has witnessed the delicate balance between love, duty, and the pursuit of dreams.

This book was not just written; it was felt. It was shaped by memories, by the sacrifices I have seen, and by the silent struggles that so many of us go through. At its heart, it is about the choices that define us—the ones that lead us forward and the ones that make us look back. Aarav's journey is deeply personal, yet it is one that belongs to everyone who has ever been at a crossroads, torn between staying and leaving, between the past and the future.

Writing this book has been an emotional experience, and I hope reading it will be just as moving. My greatest wish is that The Weight of Goodbye resonates with you, makes you pause, and perhaps even helps you find answers to questions you didn't know you had.

This book is a tribute to the sacrifices of our parents, to the resilience of the human heart, and to the moments that shape who we become.

Thank you for embarking on this journey with me.

With heartfelt appreciation,

UDIT TIWARI

Acknowledgements

Writing The Weight of Goodbye has been a journey of emotions, memories, and reflections, and I could not have completed it without the support of so many incredible people.

First and foremost, my deepest gratitude goes to my parents. Their strength, sacrifices, and unwavering belief in me have been the foundation of everything I am today. This book exists because of the values they instilled in me ,the lessons of love, resilience, and the importance of family. Every page is, in some way, a reflection of what I have learned from them.

To my friends and well-wishers who encouraged me through every stage of this book, your support means more than I can ever express. Whether it was listening to my ideas, offering feedback, or simply believing in this story when I doubted myself, you have been my pillars of strength.

A heartfelt thank you to everyone who has ever shared their life stories with me—whether knowingly or unknowingly. Your experiences, struggles, and triumphs have inspired parts of this book in ways you may never realize.

To my readers, thank you for picking up this book and stepping into Aarav's world. I hope his journey speaks to you in ways that are personal and meaningful. If this book has made you feel something, reflect, or even shed a tear, then I consider my purpose fulfilled.

And finally, to the unspoken moments, the unanswered questions, and the memories that never fade this book is for you too.

With gratitude,
UDIT TIWARI

Prologue

Some stories begin with a hello.
Some end with a goodbye.
But the ones that stay with us forever—
They are the ones caught in between.

Aarav Malhotra never imagined that a single moment, a fleeting message, or a whispered name in the quiet corners of his heart could alter the course of his life. He never thought love could be both an anchor and a storm, nor that dreams could feel as heavy as the past he carried.

He chased ambition like a man chasing the horizon, never realizing that the farther he ran, the more he lost sight of where he came from. In his search for something greater, he found love. In love, he found longing. And in longing, he discovered the ache of distance of roads diverging, of choices weighing on the soul, of goodbyes never meant to be said.

But some goodbyes are not the end. Some lead us back to where we started, to the roots we once tried to escape, to the hands that once held us, waiting for our return.

This is a story of love and loss, of ambition and sacrifice, of a heart torn between what it wants and what it needs.

But above all, this is a story of home
For sometimes, the longest journey is the one that leads us back.

1
The Roots of Home

Aarav Malhotra had always believed that the air of his hometown carried a different weight. It was thick with the scent of damp soil after early morning plowing, the fragrance of his mother's freshly made parathas, and the soft echoes of his father's voice reciting lessons to village children under the old peepal tree. His world was small but full—woven with warmth, duty, and an unspoken expectation that he, like the generations before him, would find contentment in its familiar embrace.

Nestled between rolling fields and narrow lanes where people still greeted each other by name, Aarav's town was a place where life moved at the pace of the seasons. The summer months meant the hum of ceiling fans working tirelessly against the heat, and the winters were filled with the comforting warmth of bonfires and stories passed down through generations. It was in these simple moments that Aarav had learned the values that shaped him: respect, humility, and an unwavering sense of responsibility.

His father, Hariram Malhotra, had spent his childhood tilling the land beside his own father. Their hands, cracked and hardened by years of labor, told stories of resilience and sacrifice. But Hariram had always wanted more—not for himself, but for the future. Through sheer determination, he had broken free from the cycle of farming and become a schoolteacher, earning the kind of respect that went beyond the fields. In their town, a teacher was more than just an educator; he was a guide, a figure of wisdom, and at times, the voice of reason in people's lives.

Aarav had grown up watching his father carry the weight of two worlds: one of tradition, where the land was sacred, and the other of progress, where knowledge was the key to survival. It was in the quiet moments—when Hariram sat on their modest veranda, marking students' notebooks under the dim glow of a lantern—that Aarav saw the dreams his father never spoke of. Perhaps this was why he had always felt torn between two forces: the deep-rooted values of his upbringing and the restless ambition whispering to him from beyond the fields.

Education had always been important in the Malhotra household, not as a means to escape but as a way to elevate. Aarav's mother, Sunita, though never formally schooled, was the backbone of the family's wisdom. She had a way of making sense of things, of reminding Aarav that no matter how far he went, the soil of his home would always recognize him. "Your roots will always call you back," she would say, pressing a warm chapati into his hand before he left for school.

Aarav excelled in his studies, not just out of obligation but because he saw it as his way forward. While other boys his age learned how to trade goods in the local market or planned to take over their family farms, Aarav spent his evenings under the flickering tube light, devouring books that spoke of places beyond his reach. His dreams stretched farther than the dusty roads of his town, but he was always careful never to voice them too loudly. Dreams, after all, had a way of unsettling the balance of things.

He often found solace on the roof of their house, gazing at the vast sky, wondering if there was a place where ambition and belonging could coexist. His friends would joke about his fascination with the stars, calling him a dreamer, while his father, ever the practical man, would remind him that no matter how high one soared, the ground was where a man built his home.

But Aarav's heart carried a silent conflict, one he couldn't yet put into words. He loved his home, the people, the traditions that shaped him—but something within him longed to step beyond its borders, to carve a path not already walked by those before him. The thought both excited and terrified him. Would chasing his dreams mean leaving behind everything he had ever known? Would he one day become a stranger to the place that built him?

As he lay awake that night, listening to the familiar sounds of crickets outside his window, Aarav knew one thing for certain: a choice would soon be upon him. A choice between duty and desire. Between the life that had been written for him and the one he had yet to write.

For now, though, he let himself be comforted by the nearness of home, unaware that life was already setting the stage for a decision that would change everything.

2
Echoes of Innocence

Aarav Malhotra's childhood was painted with a palette of simple joys and quiet fears. His world was a collection of small yet meaningful experiences that defined his bond with his town and its people. These were the moments that made him feel alive, but they also held the weight of an unspoken dread—the fear of leaving them behind.

One of Aarav's fondest memories was the annual kite-flying festival. Every year, the sky transformed into a canvas of vibrant colors as children and elders alike took to their rooftops. He remembered the thrill of running through the narrow lanes, clutching a spool of manjha, his hands cut by its sharp thread but his heart soaring as high as his kite. The laughter, the friendly rivalries, and the cheers when someone's kite was cut loose were etched into his soul. He knew that no skyscraper city could ever replicate the feeling of standing on a sunlit terrace, the wind in his hair, and the endless sky above him.

Then there was the evening cricket match in the village ground, where he and his friends would gather, makeshift wickets in place, with an old tennis ball that had seen better days. The game was more than just a pastime; it was a ritual, a moment of unity. He could still hear the echoes of their cheers and the playful arguments over a close run-out. The thought of never running on that familiar dusty pitch again made his chest tighten.

The local sweet shop was another place deeply ingrained in his heart. The scent of freshly fried jalebis and warm gulab jamuns filled the air as he stood in line, waiting impatiently for his turn. The shop owner, an elderly man with a kind smile, had known him since he was a toddler. "One extra for my favorite customer," he would say, slipping an additional sweet into Aarav's hand. That warmth, that familiarity—how could he ever trade it for a world where no one knew his name?

But it wasn't just the moments of joy that bound Aarav to his home. It was the quiet solace he found in the little things—the way his mother hummed an old tune while rolling chapatis, the way his father carefully folded his newspaper before setting it aside, the way the town came alive with the chimes of temple bells at dusk. These everyday details were as much a part of him as his own heartbeat.

Yet, there was an undeniable undercurrent of fear beneath it all. Every time he excelled in his studies, every time a teacher praised him for his potential, he felt the invisible push towards a future that would take him away. His ambitions whispered promises of a new world, but his heart clung to the comfort of what he had always known.

One evening, as he sat by the riverbank watching the sun dip below the horizon, Aarav voiced his fears to his childhood friend, Rohan. "What if I never come back? What if I forget what this feels like?"

Rohan skipped a stone across the water and smirked. "You won't forget. The heart remembers what the mind cannot."

Aarav smiled, but deep down, he knew that time had a way of making even the most cherished memories fade. And that, perhaps, was his greatest fear of all.

As he lay in bed that night, staring at the ceiling, he realized that every joy he experienced in his town was a thread in the fabric of his identity. The very thought of leaving felt like unraveling himself, piece by piece. But was it possible to hold onto his past while reaching for his future?

For now, he only had questions, and the answers lay in the days ahead.

3

The Weight of Freedom

As a child, Aarav had believed that freedom was the answer to everything. He had watched birds soar through the sky and wished he could follow them, untethered and unburdened by expectations. The idea of roaming far beyond the boundaries of his town filled him with an intoxicating excitement, as if the world outside held secrets meant just for him. He imagined himself walking through bustling city streets, unknown yet limitless, with no familiar voices calling him back. But the closer he got to stepping beyond those borders, the more he realized that freedom came at a cost—one that he wasn't sure he was ready to pay.

There was an evening when he had wandered a little too far from home, past the familiar fields and into the outskirts of town where the land stretched endlessly. At first, he felt a thrill—an exhilarating rush of discovery. But soon, a strange unease settled in his chest. The trees seemed taller, their shadows stretching longer in the dimming light, and the silence felt unfamiliar, almost eerie. For the first time, he felt the absence of familiarity—no voices calling his name, no comforting sights of home. He turned back, suddenly aware of how small he was in the vastness of the world. That night, as he lay in bed, staring at the ceiling, he questioned whether the vastness he had craved would one day swallow him whole.

The unpredictability of life had always felt unfair to him. He had seen how quickly things changed—how one moment could alter the course of everything. When his neighbor, an old storyteller, passed away, Aarav had felt a strange hollowness. The stories that once painted his childhood nights were now gone, leaving behind only echoes in his mind. He had sat outside the old man's house, waiting as if he might still hear one last tale carried by the wind. The realization struck him hard: people left, moments faded, and nothing stayed the same.

There was also the day his childhood friend Ravi moved to the city. They had spent every summer racing through the fields, climbing trees, and sneaking mangoes from the orchards. They had promised to write to each other, but over time, the letters became fewer, the words shorter, until one day, they simply stopped. Ravi had moved on, and Aarav was left behind, grappling with the understanding that even the strongest bonds could fade with distance.

Despite being surrounded by family and friends, Aarav often found himself feeling lonely. He was never truly alone, yet there was an emptiness he couldn't explain. He would watch his parents share quiet glances of understanding, his friends laughing about things he sometimes couldn't relate to, and he would wonder if he was drifting further away from them without even meaning to. He wanted to be part of their world, yet a part of him longed for something else—something he couldn't quite define.

On one particular afternoon, he sat by the riverbank, tossing pebbles into the water, lost in thought. His sister, Rashmi, sat beside him and nudged his shoulder. "You look like you're carrying the weight of the whole world, Aarav."

He sighed, struggling to find the right words. "I just... I don't know if I belong here forever. But leaving feels just as difficult as staying."

rashmi chuckled softly, gazing at the rippling water. "That's the thing about life, isn't it? No matter where you go, a part of you will always belong to where you started."

Her words stayed with him long after that day, lingering in his mind like a song he couldn't forget. He realized that while he longed for freedom, he feared what it would take from him. The warmth of home, the certainty of knowing his place, the comfort of never having to wonder where he truly belonged.

One evening, as he helped his mother roll out chapatis, he asked her, "Do you ever wish you had seen more of the world?"

She smiled, tucking a loose strand of hair behind her ear. "I see the world through all of you. Your father in his books, rashmi in her stories, and you... you in your endless questions."

Aarav thought about her words as he watched the steam rise from the hot bread. Did he want to see the world for himself, or did he simply want to know if he could? Was he searching for adventure, or was he just afraid of regret?

For now, he would savor the days he had left in his town—the laughter of his friends, the warmth of his home, the familiar rhythm of life. But deep inside, he knew—sooner or later—he would have to choose between the longing for something greater and the fear of losing what he already had.

4
Echoes of Change

Aarav stood at the edge of the town's main road, watching as a bus rumbled past, kicking up a swirl of dust in its wake. He often found himself here, lingering near the crossroads, as if caught between the past and the future. Every so often, he would see someone from his town leave, their eyes bright with the anticipation of something greater, their expressions shadowed with uncertainty. He wondered if he, too, would one day be among them, carrying only a bag full of dreams and a heart heavy with hesitation.

His father often spoke about responsibility, about how a man's duty was to his roots. "The city will offer you many things, Aarav, but it will never give you a home. That, you already have." Aarav respected his father's wisdom, but he couldn't shake the feeling that there was more to life than familiarity. He wanted to see the world beyond the fields and narrow lanes, to understand what lay past the comforting predictability of home. Yet, the thought of leaving behind the laughter of his younger sister, the aroma of his mother's evening chai, and the knowing nods of the shopkeepers who had seen him grow up, made his chest tighten.

One evening, as he walked through the marketplace, he met an old acquaintance, Suraj, who had moved to the city for his studies. Suraj had returned for a brief visit, but something about him had changed. His posture was straighter, his words carried an air of confidence that Aarav couldn't quite place.

"So, Aarav," Suraj said, adjusting the strap of his sleek leather bag, "still dreaming about the big city?"

Aarav hesitated before replying, "More than ever. But dreaming and leaving are two different things."

Suraj nodded knowingly. "That's true. Leaving isn't easy. But neither is staying, when your heart is somewhere else."

They spoke for a while, reminiscing about childhood pranks and schoolyard fights. But beneath the nostalgia, Aarav felt a strange disconnect. Suraj's words hinted at something unspoken—a gap between the boy who had left and the one who had stayed. The easy camaraderie of their youth now carried an invisible weight.

That night, he climbed onto the roof of his house, lying back against the cool tiles, staring up at the endless sky. The stars were scattered like distant lanterns, each one carrying a possibility he had yet to explore. He thought about his childhood, about the days spent chasing dragonflies in the fields, about the evenings spent by the river with his friends, their laughter echoing against the water. Those memories were warm and comforting, but they also felt like anchors, holding him in place when the tide of life wanted to pull him forward.

He recalled the annual town fair, the way the scent of freshly fried jalebis filled the air, and how he and his friends would race to win cheap plastic toys from game stalls. He thought about the temple bells ringing in the early morning, the collective prayers of the town, and how even the smallest joys seemed magnified in their simplicity. Would he ever find that sense of belonging elsewhere?

His mother found him there sometime later, her presence as gentle as the evening breeze. "You've been quiet lately," she observed, sitting down beside him.

Aarav sighed. "Ma, do you ever wonder what life could have been like if you had left? If you had chosen something different?"

She smiled, tucking a loose strand of hair behind her ear. "Perhaps. But I chose this life because I found my happiness here. Happiness isn't about where you are, Aarav—it's about who you are when you get there."

Her words settled deep within him, but they did not quiet the restless longing inside his heart. The fear of losing what he loved battled against the desire to see what lay beyond. He was a son of this land, tied to its traditions, yet he felt the pull of the unknown, beckoning him toward something greater.

For now, all he could do was wait and listen—to the echoes of change that whispered to him in the quiet moments, to the road that stretched before him, waiting for the day he would finally take his first step away from home.

5

The Crossroads of Fate

The days that followed were a blur of routine, yet Aarav felt an undercurrent of change humming beneath the surface of his everyday life. The streets of his town, once comforting in their predictability, now felt smaller, as if the world beyond them was beckoning him louder than ever before.

One afternoon, as he walked back from the market, he found himself stopping at the railway station. It wasn't a place he frequented, but something about it always intrigued him. The sound of trains pulling in and out, the distant chatter of passengers, and the rhythmic announcements over the speakers made him feel as if he were standing at the edge of two different worlds—the known and the unknown.

He sat on one of the wooden benches, watching people come and go. A young boy clung to his mother's saree, his eyes wide with excitement as he pointed at a passing train. A group of students, laughing and chattering, boarded a carriage, their hands clutching books and packed lunches. An elderly man, dressed in a simple kurta, stared out at the tracks as if lost in time.

Aarav wondered what their stories were. Were they leaving behind homes like his? Were they running towards a dream, or away from something they feared?

His thoughts were interrupted when he felt a gentle tap on his shoulder. He turned to see an old teacher of his, Mr. Verma, standing there with a knowing smile. "Aarav, my boy, lost in thought again?"

Aarav smiled sheepishly. "Just thinking about things, sir."

Mr. Verma sat beside him, placing his walking stick between his knees. "You remind me of myself when I was your age. Always looking at the horizon, wondering if there's something more beyond it."

Aarav chuckled. "And did you find it?"

The old man nodded, his eyes filled with nostalgia. "In a way, yes. I left this town once, just like many others. But no matter where I went, I carried a part of it with me. You see, Aarav, leaving isn't about running away—it's about discovering yourself in a different place."

Aarav absorbed his words, feeling the weight of them settle in his chest.

That evening, as he walked home, the sky painted in hues of orange and pink, he realized something—his hesitation wasn't just about leaving. It was about proving to himself that he was capable of more than just dreaming. It was about facing the unknown, despite the fear that clung to him.

As he approached his house, he saw his father standing by the doorway, a quiet strength in his posture. Aarav knew he would have to talk to him soon, to tell him about the decisions stirring within his heart. But for now, he let himself breathe in the familiarity of home, knowing that the crossroads of fate were closer than ever before.

6
The Echoes of Goodbye

The days that followed were heavier than Aarav had anticipated. Every routine, every conversation, every small moment felt magnified, as if his heart was imprinting the memories before he had to let them go. The laughter of the children playing in the alleyways, the rustling of the old neem tree outside his window, the scent of his mother's spices lingering in the air—all of it felt like a bittersweet melody he never wanted to forget.

One evening, as he walked through the narrow streets of his town, he found himself stopping at the small tea stall where he had spent countless evenings with his friends. The owner, an old man with wrinkled hands and a kind smile, greeted him with a knowing nod.

"Aarav beta, your usual?" he asked, already pouring a cup of steaming chai.

Aarav smiled as he took the cup, the warmth seeping into his hands. He glanced around, the wooden benches worn from years of conversations, laughter, and the weight of shared worries. Tonight, they sat empty, as if waiting for the past to return.

As he sipped his tea, a familiar voice called out. "Planning to leave without a proper goodbye?"

It was Rohit, his closest friend since childhood, the one who had seen him through every phase of his life. Aarav chuckled, shaking his head. "Would you let me?"

Rohit sat beside him, his tone turning serious. "It's strange, isn't it? How we spend years in one place thinking it'll always be the same, only to realize one day that change was inevitable all along."

Aarav sighed, stirring his tea absentmindedly. "I thought I was ready. But the closer I get to leaving, the harder it feels."

Rohit leaned back, looking up at the sky. "Because home isn't just a place, Aarav. It's people. It's moments. And no matter how far you go, you'll always carry it with you."

As they sat in silence, the weight of their words settled between them. The memories of their childhood—stealing mangoes from the neighbor's tree, racing their bicycles down the narrow streets, whispering about their dreams under the open sky—came rushing back, making the moment even harder to let go of.

That night, as Aarav walked home, his mother was waiting at the doorstep, just like she always did. She placed a gentle hand on his cheek, her eyes searching his.

"You've always been my brave boy," she whispered. "But no matter where you go, you'll always have a home here."

A lump formed in Aarav's throat, but he nodded. He wanted to tell her everything he felt—that he was scared, that he would miss her, that a part of him wished he could stay—but no words seemed enough.

The next morning, he visited the fields where his father often spent his time, watching over the land that had provided for their family for generations. Hariram Malhotra stood quietly, his hands resting on his walking stick, his gaze fixed on the horizon.

"You know," his father said, not turning to look at him, "when I left farming to become a teacher, people said I was abandoning my roots. But I wasn't. I was just finding a new way to honor them."

Aarav swallowed hard, understanding the unspoken message in his father's words. He wasn't leaving his home behind—he was carrying it forward.

As he lay in bed that night, staring at the ceiling, he realized that leaving wasn't just about stepping into the unknown. It was about carrying the echoes of goodbye, the love of those who had shaped

him, and the promise that some things would never truly be left
behind.

7
Crossroads of Fate

The day of departure loomed closer, and with it came an unfamiliar restlessness that clung to Aarav like a shadow. The town, which had once felt like a comforting embrace, now seemed to tighten around him, pulling him back just as he was about to leave. The thought of walking away from everything he had ever known sent a strange chill down his spine. Was he truly ready to trade familiarity for the unknown?

His mother had been unusually quiet, her once relentless chatter replaced with long, thoughtful silences. Aarav found her one evening, standing at the entrance of their home, her hands clutching the ends of her dupatta as she gazed out at the street.

"Ma?" he called softly.

She turned, forcing a smile that didn't quite reach her eyes. "You'll write to me, won't you?"

Aarav felt his throat tighten. "Every week."

She nodded, as if trying to believe him. "I keep thinking about the first time you walked to school alone. You were so excited to be independent, but by the evening, you came running back home, crying." She chuckled, but there was a sadness in it. "I wonder if it'll be the same this time."

Aarav wanted to assure her that he wouldn't come running back, but deep down, a part of him feared she might be right.

Later that evening, he found himself wandering towards the old banyan tree where he and his childhood friends used to gather. To his surprise, a group of them were already there—Rohit, Meera, and a few others—sitting around an old transistor playing a nostalgic song from their school days. They looked up as he approached, and for a moment, it felt like nothing had changed.

"We figured you'd come here one last time," Rohit said, patting the empty spot next to him.

Aarav sank down, running his fingers over the exposed roots of the banyan. "I don't know how to say goodbye."

Meera gave him a playful nudge. "Then don't. Just say 'see you later.'"

They sat in comfortable silence, each lost in their own thoughts. It was Rohit who finally broke it. "You know, Aarav, we always thought you'd be the first one to leave this place. But now that it's actually happening, it feels... weird."

Aarav exhaled, leaning back against the tree. "It feels weird to me too."

For a while, they reminisced about the past—the time they sneaked into a wedding for free food, the cricket matches played under the scorching sun, the countless evenings spent debating what their futures would hold. The laughter came easily, but underneath it lay the heavy realization that this chapter of their lives was coming to an end.

Then, as if fate itself wanted to remind Aarav of what he was leaving behind, a sudden commotion broke the tranquility of the night. A frantic voice echoed through the street—an old neighbor was calling for help. Aarav and his friends rushed towards the sound and found Mr. Sharma, the kind bookseller, clutching his chest in pain.

Without hesitation, Aarav and Rohit helped him onto a bicycle, with Aarav pedaling as fast as he could towards the nearest clinic. The rush, the desperation, the fear of losing someone familiar—it was all a reminder of how deeply he was woven into the fabric of this town.

After ensuring Mr. Sharma received the necessary treatment, Aarav stood outside the clinic, catching his breath. Rohit placed a hand on his shoulder. "You're leaving, but a part of you will always belong here. And that's okay."

Aarav nodded, staring at the town he had always called home. It had given him everything—his childhood, his friendships, his values. But as much as it tried to pull him back, his dreams lay ahead, beyond the familiar roads and faces.

He realized then that leaving didn't mean forgetting. It didn't mean severing ties. It simply meant carrying home with him, wherever he went.

And so, as the first light of dawn crept over the horizon, Aarav stood at the crossroads of fate, ready to take the next step.

8
The First Step

The morning of Aarav's departure arrived with a surreal stillness. The town, usually alive with the sounds of early risers and street vendors, felt muted in his ears. Every detail seemed amplified—the creak of the old wooden door, the rustling of leaves in the courtyard, the faint aroma of his mother's chai brewing in the kitchen. The familiarity of these small moments made his chest tighten with emotions he wasn't prepared to confront.

He dressed slowly, his hands lingering on familiar objects—a well-worn book, a cricket bat with faded signatures, a photograph of his family from a festival years ago. These weren't just things; they were pieces of his childhood, reminders of a life he was about to leave behind. Each object had a story, a memory attached. The cricket bat still carried the laughter of summer evenings spent with friends, the book held scribbled notes from his late-night studies, and the photograph was a frozen moment of happiness he wished he could step back into.

His mother stood by the doorway, watching him with a quiet sadness. Her eyes, though warm, had a certain glassy sheen to them, as if holding back unshed tears. "I packed some sweets for you," she said, placing a small metal box in his bag. "For when you miss home."

Aarav managed a smile. "I'll miss you more." His voice wavered slightly, betraying the turmoil inside him.

His father, ever the reserved one, cleared his throat and handed him an envelope. "For emergencies," he muttered. But Aarav knew it was more than that—it was his father's way of saying he cared, even if words failed him.

Aarav hesitated before reaching out and touching his father's feet—a gesture of respect he had done countless times before, yet this time, it felt different. His father placed a firm hand on his shoulder, an unspoken blessing passing between them.

Outside, Rohit and Meera were waiting by the bus stop. "Look at you, all grown up," Meera teased, nudging him. Rohit smirked. "Don't get too used to the city life. We'll drag you back for every festival."

Aarav laughed, but there was a heaviness in his chest. Leaving wasn't just about stepping into a new world—it was about carrying the weight of the old one with him. Every street he had walked a thousand times before suddenly seemed to hold more meaning. The shopkeeper who always gave him an extra toffee, the neighbors who asked about his studies, the small temple where he had whispered his wishes as a child—all of it was a part of him, a world he was walking away from.

As the bus arrived, he turned back for one last glance. His mother's eyes glistened, his father gave a barely perceptible nod, and his friends stood with lopsided grins, trying to mask their own emotions. He wanted to memorize this moment, to etch it deep into his soul. The fear of forgetting even the smallest detail terrified him.

He took a deep breath and stepped onto the bus. The door shut behind him with a finality that sent a shiver down his spine. The engine rumbled, and the town he had known all his life began to fade into the distance.

As the fields and houses blurred past the window, memories flooded his mind—the way the monsoon rains drenched the streets, the sound of his mother humming while cooking, the warmth of the summer nights spent on the rooftop counting stars. Would the city ever feel like home the way this place did? Would he still be the same Aarav once he left?

Aarav wasn't sure what awaited him beyond the horizon. But for the first time, the fear of the unknown was matched by the thrill of possibility. He clutched the envelope his father had given him, a symbol of his parents' quiet but unwavering support, and exhaled slowly.

And so, with one last look at his fading home, Aarav took his first step into the future.

9
Echoes of Departure

The bus had long disappeared down the dusty road, but Hariram and Sunita stood at the gate, their eyes fixed on the vanishing horizon as if hoping time would grant them a few more moments with their son. The house, which had always felt full with Aarav's presence, now seemed unnaturally silent. Even the chirping of birds in the neem tree outside couldn't fill the void left behind.

Sunita, who had held back her tears while Aarav was still within sight, finally let them flow as she turned back towards the house. The kitchen, which had been filled with his chatter every morning, now felt emptier. She absentmindedly reached for the extra cup she always set out for him before realizing he wouldn't be there to drink it. A lump formed in her throat.

Hariram, on the other hand, sat on the veranda with his usual cup of tea, staring at the ground, his thoughts miles away. He wasn't a man of many words, but the absence of his son left a weight on his chest that he couldn't quite shake. He had always known this day would come, that Aarav's dreams were bigger than their small town, but knowing didn't make it any easier.

"Do you think he will eat on time?" Sunita asked, breaking the silence.

Hariram exhaled slowly. "He'll manage. He's not a child anymore." But his voice lacked conviction.

"He may not be a child, but he's still our son," Sunita whispered, running her fingers over the edge of the metal lunchbox she had packed for Aarav. She had filled it with his favorite sweets, hoping it would remind him of home, of love that never wavered no matter the distance.

Meanwhile, miles away, Aarav sat by the window of the bus, his forehead pressed against the glass, watching the landscape shift from familiar fields to the unknown roads ahead. His heart was heavy, but he couldn't quite place the emotion. Was it sadness? Fear? Excitement? Or an overwhelming mix of all three?

His mind replayed the morning's events—his mother's lingering touch on his shoulder, his father's silent nod, the teasing but supportive words of Rohit and Meera. Each memory carried weight, pressing down on him as if he had left a part of himself behind with them.

For years, he had dreamed of this moment, of stepping out into a world larger than the one he had known. But now that it was happening, he felt strangely uprooted. The independence he had longed for felt less like freedom and more like a burden. The thought of waking up in a place where no one would call his name in the morning, where the air wouldn't carry the scent of home-cooked meals, sent an unfamiliar chill through him.

Aarav reached into his bag and pulled out the envelope his father had given him. He ran his fingers over its edges, debating whether to open it now or wait. It wasn't about the money inside; it was about what it represented—his father's unspoken emotions, his silent way of saying he believed in him. Tucking it safely back, Aarav sighed.

A new journey awaited him, but he was beginning to understand that leaving home was not just about distance—it was about carrying the weight of everything and everyone left behind. The real challenge wasn't just finding success in a new city; it was learning how to exist in a world where home was now a memory instead of a presence.

Back at home, as night fell, Sunita found herself walking into Aarav's room, running her fingers over his study table, adjusting the slightly crooked photo frame of their last festival together. Hariram stood by the door, watching her, a deep sigh escaping his lips.

"He'll be fine," he said, more to himself than to her.

Sunita nodded but didn't turn around. "I know," she whispered. "But will we?"

And in that quiet house, where every corner held a memory of their son, they both realized that while Aarav had taken his first step into the future, they were left standing in the echoes of his departure.

10
The Struggle

The city was nothing like home. The streets pulsed with restless energy, cars honked impatiently, and the air smelled of possibilities mixed with pollution. Aarav had imagined this life countless times, yet standing in the middle of it now, he felt like an outsider looking in. The tall buildings, the hurried faces, the absence of familiar voices—it was overwhelming.

His first few days were spent adjusting to the smallest of things: waking up to an alarm instead of his mother's voice, eating food that lacked the warmth of home-cooked meals, navigating streets where no one smiled in greeting. The loneliness hit him hardest at night when the silence of his small rented room reminded him of everything he had left behind.

Back home, his parents were feeling the emptiness too. Sunita had developed a habit of setting an extra plate at the table before catching herself. Hariram, though outwardly composed, found himself staring at Aarav's old books, flipping through pages filled with scribbled notes and dreams. The house had lost its liveliness, and the town felt smaller without Aarav's presence.

Meanwhile, in the city, Aarav was facing a different battle. College life was fast-paced, filled with students who seemed to have everything figured out. He often found himself questioning if he truly belonged here. The very ambition that had brought him to this place now felt like a heavy burden. Professors expected brilliance, classmates exuded confidence, and the competitive air was suffocating.

One evening, after a particularly difficult day of lectures and endless assignments, he sat alone at a tea stall near his hostel. The warm cup in his hands reminded him of the chai his mother used to make. It was a small comfort in an otherwise chaotic world.

"First time away from home?" The chai vendor, an old man with kind eyes, asked as he handed Aarav a biscuit.

Aarav hesitated before nodding.

The old man chuckled. "It gets easier. But never quite feels the same."

His words struck a chord. Aarav had assumed that time would erase the ache of separation, but now he wasn't so sure. Was this struggle temporary? Or was this what growing up truly meant—constantly longing for a place you could never fully return to?

His challenges didn't end there. Financial worries loomed over him. Though his father had given him some money, Aarav knew he had to be careful. Expenses piled up quickly, and he felt guilty every time he had to call home and ask for more. He tried taking up tutoring, helping students who struggled with mathematics, but balancing work and studies drained him further.

And then there was the self-doubt.

Back in his town, he had been among the brightest. Here, he was just one among thousands, all fighting for the same dreams. There were moments when he wanted to give up, to return home, to escape the pressure. But every time the thought crossed his mind, he remembered his father's silent nod, his mother's hopeful eyes, and the sacrifices they had made to send him here.

Aarav wasn't just fighting for himself. He was fighting for them too.

One evening, as he sat on his small balcony, looking at the city lights, he thought about choice. He had chosen to be here. He had chosen ambition over comfort. But choice came with struggles, and struggles came with growth.

For the first time in weeks, he allowed himself to believe that maybe—just maybe—he would find his place here. That the struggle, however painful, was part of the journey.

Back home, as Sunita folded Aarav's old clothes and Hariram prepared his lesson plans, they too realized something—this pain, this longing, was not a sign of weakness. It was the price of love, of raising a son with dreams too big for their small town.

And so, in different worlds, separated by miles but connected by love, both Aarav and his parents braced themselves for the long road ahead.

11

Crossroads

The city had begun to feel less foreign, but the battle inside Aarav remained. Days blurred into nights filled with assignments, part-time tutoring, and silent walks back to his hostel. He had found a routine, but he had yet to find his rhythm. There were moments when he felt invincible, ready to conquer every challenge thrown his way, and then there were days when exhaustion and loneliness weighed him down, making him question everything.

One evening, as he sat by his hostel window, staring at the city lights, he received a call from home. It was his mother.

"How are you, beta?" she asked, her voice carrying the warmth of home.

"I'm good, Maa. Just busy with studies," he replied, forcing a cheerfulness he didn't quite feel.

"Are you eating properly? You sound tired."

Aarav swallowed the lump in his throat. She always knew.

"I am, Maa. Don't worry."

There was a pause. Then, in a softer voice, she said, "Your father misses you. He doesn't say it, but I know."

Aarav clenched his fist. He missed them too. More than he could put into words. He wanted to tell her that some nights, he lay awake longing for the sounds of his small town, for the comfort of his home. But he couldn't. Instead, he simply said, "Tell him I miss him too."

The call ended, but the weight in his chest remained. He lay back on his bed, staring at the ceiling, feeling the silent battle within him grow louder. He had always known that leaving home wouldn't be easy, but he hadn't realized just how deeply his roots pulled at him.

As he tried to shake off his emotions, an unexpected text flashed on his screen. It was from Meera.

Meera: "Hey city boy, how's life? Or should I ask if you've turned into a proper 'suit-boot wala' yet?"

Aarav chuckled. Trust Meera to pull him out of his thoughts. He quickly typed back.

Aarav: "Not quite. Still the same old Aarav, just surrounded by taller buildings."

They chatted for a while, reminiscing about old times, teasing each other like nothing had changed. But deep down, Aarav knew things had changed. And they would continue to change. He wanted to hold onto his past, but the future was knocking louder each day.

The next day, Aarav found himself sitting in the college library, staring at an email from a senior. It was about an internship opportunity—his first real step into the world he had dreamt of. It was everything he had worked for, yet a part of him hesitated. Taking this meant pushing himself further, stepping deeper into a life that was pulling him away from home. Was he ready for that? Could he embrace this new world without losing the boy who once sat under a peepal tree, listening to his father teach?

Later that evening, he called Rohit.

"Bhai, tell me honestly—do you ever feel like we're losing parts of ourselves by being here?"

Rohit was silent for a moment before replying, "Maybe. But isn't that how we grow? By letting go of some things to make space for others?"

Aarav exhaled. Growth. Change. Choices. How much did one have to sacrifice for the other?

That night, he sat by his window again, looking at the city that once felt intimidating but now felt... possible. He thought about his father's sacrifices, his mother's unwavering faith in him, the friends who still anchored him to his past, and the future that lay ahead. He imagined his father sitting on their veranda, marking students' notebooks under the dim glow of a lantern. He imagined his mother pressing warm chapatis into his hand, telling him that his roots would always call him back. He imagined the dusty roads of home, the familiar faces that made his world whole. And then, he imagined a future he had yet to build.

Aarav Malhotra was at a crossroads. He didn't have all the answers yet, but for the first time, he wasn't afraid of the questions.

With a deep breath, he clicked on the email and typed his response.

"Dear Sir, I would like to apply for the internship...".

12
The Ties That Bind

Aarav had expected the internship to be challenging, but he hadn't anticipated the whirlwind it would become. Days stretched into late nights, filled with deadlines, research, and meetings that made him feel like he was finally stepping into the world he had always envisioned. He thrived on the fast pace, the rush of productivity, the satisfaction of proving himself. Yet, with each step forward, he felt a faint but persistent tug—like an invisible thread connecting him to the life he had left behind.

It started with small things: missing a festival at home, forgetting to return a call, feeling out of place when he finally spoke to his parents. His father, always composed, sounded distant. His mother, ever warm, spoke of home as though it were a place he had outgrown. And then there was Meera.

They had continued their sporadic conversations—sometimes playful, sometimes deep—but there was something in her tone lately that made him uneasy. One evening, she sent a message that lingered in his mind longer than he liked.

Meera: "You ever feel like we're all just drifting? Like no matter how much we try to hold on, things are slipping?"

Aarav stared at his phone, fingers hovering over the keyboard. He wanted to tell her he felt the same, that he wasn't sure where 'home' even was anymore. Instead, he typed:

Aarav: "Maybe. Or maybe we're just scared of letting go."

She didn't reply. And that silence gnawed at him.

The following week, he received a call from his father. It was brief, direct, with none of the usual pleasantries.

"There's a wedding coming up in the family," his father said. "You should try to come."

Aarav hesitated. He had another big presentation coming up, and the thought of stepping away—even for a few days—felt impossible.

"I'll try, Baba," he said, knowing that 'try' wasn't the answer his father wanted to hear.

A beat of silence, then, "Your mother would like to see you."

It was enough to make his heart clench. He promised to think about it.

That night, as he walked back to his hostel, something shifted in him. The city had become familiar, but it would never be home. The weight of everything—his dreams, his responsibilities, the people waiting for him—felt heavier than ever.

He recalled the memories of his childhood—the late-night storytelling sessions with his mother, the evenings spent chasing fireflies with his friends, the pride in his father's eyes when he had won his first academic award. Those moments were more than just nostalgia; they were pieces of himself he had unknowingly left behind. The thought unsettled him.

When he reached his room, he found a small note slipped under his door. It was from Rohit.

"Bhai, stop running in circles. Go home before it's too late."

Aarav sat on his bed, staring at the note for a long time. He had been convincing himself that moving forward meant leaving behind the past, but maybe the two weren't mutually exclusive. Maybe he didn't have to choose between ambition and belonging.

That night, sleep evaded him. He found himself scrolling through old photos on his phone—pictures of his family, the streets of his hometown, the little celebrations they used to have over the smallest victories. His heart ached at the thought of how much had changed, and how much he had allowed himself to drift away.

The next morning, he woke up with a decision made. He called his boss, explained that he needed to take a few days off, and then booked his ticket home. As the train rumbled forward, carrying him back to where he had begun, he wondered if he would still fit into the world he had left behind—or if home had changed in his absence.

As he neared his destination, his phone buzzed. It was Meera.

Meera: "You finally stopped running?"

A small smile tugged at his lips. Maybe he had. Maybe he was finally ready to face what he had been avoiding all along.

With a deep breath, he picked up his phone and dialed home.

"Maa," he said softly when she answered. "I'm coming home."

13

Homecoming

The train ride home was longer than Aarav remembered. Each passing mile felt like peeling back the layers of time, bringing him closer to the world he had left behind. He leaned against the window, watching fields blur into towns, towns into villages, until familiarity began to settle into his bones. The landscape hadn't changed much—the same quiet roads, the same small stations where hawkers called out for tea and snacks—but something within him had.

Aarav had spent years longing to break free from this place, to escape its predictability. Now, as he neared home, he felt a strange mix of comfort and unease. Would he still fit in here? Would his family see him the same way? Had he changed too much—or worse, had he not changed at all?

As the train pulled into the station, he spotted his father standing on the platform. Hariram Malhotra looked older, the lines on his face deeper than Aarav remembered. His posture was still upright, but there was something weary in his eyes. Aarav hesitated for a second before stepping off, his bag slung over his shoulder.

His father's expression didn't change much, but there was warmth in his eyes. "You've grown thinner," he said simply, his voice carrying both concern and quiet approval.

Aarav managed a small smile. "City life."

They walked toward home in near silence, the familiar scent of earth and evening fires filling the air. The streets were alive with children playing, shopkeepers closing up, neighbors exchanging end-of-day stories. Every person who crossed their path greeted his father with respect. Aarav had once taken that for granted, but now he saw it differently. His father wasn't just a teacher; he was a pillar of the community.

As they neared their house, the wooden door creaked open before they even reached it. His mother stood there, eyes scanning him as though memorizing his face all over again. Then, without a word, she pulled him into a tight embrace. The scent of home—turmeric, incense, and the faint sweetness of freshly made kheer—wrapped around him.

"You've been gone too long," she whispered.

That night, as he sat at the dinner table, he felt the weight of time. His father asked about work, his mother insisted he eat more, and his younger cousin bombarded him with questions about city life. It was all familiar, yet it felt distant, as if he were watching a version of his life that once belonged to him but no longer did.

Later, he stepped outside into the quiet courtyard. The night sky here was clearer than in the city, the stars stretching endlessly above him. He thought of Meera's words—how things slipped no matter how tightly you held on. He thought of the unspoken words between him and his father, the lingering emotions in his mother's embrace, the laughter of his childhood that now seemed like echoes in the wind.

Aarav wasn't sure what he had expected from this visit, but the depth of emotion caught him off guard. There was warmth, nostalgia, even relief—but also guilt. He saw it in his mother's lingering glances, in his father's silent observations. They had supported his dreams, but had he, in his pursuit, unknowingly distanced himself from them?

The next morning, he was woken up early by the distant sound of temple bells and the rhythmic sweeping of the courtyard. As he stepped outside, he found his mother already at work, preparing tea.

She looked up and smiled, patting the wooden bench beside her.

"Come, have chai with me," she said, pouring the steaming liquid into two clay cups.

Aarav sat down, taking in the peaceful surroundings—the familiar voices of neighbors chatting, the scent of damp earth after the morning watering, the way the sunlight painted golden streaks through the trees. He had missed this, more than he realized.

His mother stirred her tea absentmindedly. "You're quiet," she noted.

Aarav hesitated, then sighed. "I don't know, Maa. It feels like everything's changed, but at the same time, nothing has."

She chuckled softly, her eyes wise. "That's how life works. The place remains, but we change. The people stay, but their hearts carry different stories."

Aarav nodded, letting her words sink in. His father stepped out a few minutes later, holding a newspaper. He gave Aarav a glance before sitting down across from them.

"You'll be visiting the school today?" his father asked, more as a statement than a question.

Aarav knew there was no avoiding it. The school had been such a huge part of his father's life, and now, the weight of that legacy felt heavier than ever. "Yes," he said, sipping his tea.

His father gave a small nod of approval, but there was something more in his gaze—something unreadable.

The rest of the morning passed in a haze of greetings and familiar faces. The townspeople treated Aarav like a son who had returned after a great battle, their warmth both overwhelming and comforting. He realized how much he had been missed, how much people still saw him as a part of this place. Yet, with every warm handshake and nostalgic conversation, the question remained in his mind—was he here to stay, or was this just another fleeting visit?

As he stood in front of the school gates, watching children run past him with books clutched to their chests, he felt it again—that pull between two worlds. He had left to chase a dream, but he had never considered what he might be leaving behind in the process.

Aarav wasn't sure of the answers yet. But for now, he let himself breathe in the air of home, feeling its warmth settle deep within him.

Tomorrow, there would be more conversations, more expectations, more questions. But tonight, he was just a son returning home.

14
:Unfolding Threads

The wedding preparations had transformed the house into a whirlwind of colors, sounds, and endless chatter. Aarav had barely stepped in before he was swept up in the chaos. His mother, thrilled by his presence, had immediately put him to work—stringing garlands, carrying trays of sweets, and entertaining distant relatives who fussed over how much he had grown. It was a familiar disarray, the kind that once made him impatient but now filled him with an unexpected warmth.

The scent of marigolds and rosewater mixed with the aromas of rich, ghee-laden sweets. Women bustled about in bright sarees, their bangles clinking as they worked, while the men debated loudly over wedding logistics. Children ran through the courtyard, giggling and slipping through the gaps between people like little whirlwinds of joy. This was home—messy, loud, and impossibly alive.

Amidst the endless stream of guests was Aisha, a distant cousin of the bride. Aarav first noticed her standing near the entrance, effortlessly balancing a tray of sweets while dodging a group of running children. Her quiet confidence intrigued him. Unlike the others, she didn't seem lost in the frenzy; instead, she moved through it as if she belonged to a different rhythm. Their eyes met briefly, and she offered him a polite nod before disappearing into the house.

Later that evening, as Aarav wrestled with a tangled mess of fairy lights on the veranda, Aisha appeared beside him.

"You don't look like you belong here," she observed, leaning against a pillar with a teasing smirk.

Aarav raised an eyebrow. "Is it that obvious?"

She tilted her head. "You have the look of someone whose mind is somewhere else."

He glanced at the half-lit courtyard, then back at her. "Maybe. Or maybe I'm just trying to figure out where I do belong."

She hummed thoughtfully, her gaze unwavering. "Do you think you'll find your answer at this wedding?"

Aarav chuckled. "Doubtful. But at least the food's good."

Aisha laughed, the sound light and genuine. "That's a fair reason to be here."

Over the next few days, Aarav and Aisha found themselves crossing paths often—during meal preparations, between ceremonies, in the quiet pockets of time when the festivities momentarily slowed. She was unlike anyone he had met. There was no forced politeness, no meaningless chatter. She spoke with clarity, as if she had already made peace with the choices in her life. For someone like Aarav, who was still tangled in uncertainty, that was both fascinating and unsettling.

One afternoon, as Aarav helped carry chairs for the evening's mehendi function, he overheard a conversation between his uncle and father.

"He's been away too long," his uncle muttered. "The city changes people. You'll see, he won't stay."

His father's voice was steady but quiet. "Let him decide where his path leads. He carries this home with him, no matter where he goes."

Aarav turned away before they could see him listening, his heart tightening. He wondered if his father truly believed that—or if he was simply preparing himself for the inevitable.

That night, as the courtyard shimmered with golden lights and the sangeet began, Aarav found himself sitting beside Aisha on the steps. The elders danced in the center, their laughter and claps blending seamlessly with the rhythmic beats of the dhol. It was a kind of joy that belonged to simpler times, untouched by the weight of choices and expectations.

"You look lost in thought again," Aisha said, nudging him slightly.

He exhaled, a small smile playing on his lips. "Just thinking about how life keeps moving, even when you're not ready for it."

She glanced at him, her expression unreadable. "Maybe that's the point. Maybe we're never supposed to be fully ready."

Aarav turned to her, studying the way the lanterns reflected in her dark eyes. He didn't know if he would ever be fully ready to make the choices that loomed ahead of him. But in that moment, sitting beside Aisha with the hum of music and laughter filling the night, he allowed himself to just be present.

15

The Weight of Choices

The wedding celebrations had begun to wind down, leaving behind a lingering warmth in the air. The house, once filled with vibrant chaos, now carried the weight of inevitable goodbyes. Relatives packed their bags, elders rested after days of festivities, and the younger ones clung to the last few hours of shared laughter and whispered conversations.

Aarav sat on the terrace, gazing at the open fields stretching beyond the horizon. The stars blinked above him, unchanged and unmoving, yet everything within him felt like it was shifting. He had always believed that leaving home was a necessity, that the city was where his dreams belonged, but now, a quiet ache settled in his chest, making him question everything.

"Escaping the crowd?" Aisha's voice cut through the quiet.

He turned to see her standing by the doorway, her silhouette outlined by the dim light from the hall. She stepped closer, wrapping her shawl around her shoulders against the cool night breeze.

"Something like that," he admitted. "Needed a moment to breathe."

Aisha sat down beside him, pulling her knees to her chest. "So, when do you leave?"

"Tomorrow morning." The words felt heavier than he had expected.

She nodded, staring at the distant flicker of a lantern in the fields. "And are you ready?"

He exhaled slowly. "I don't know if I'll ever be."

Silence stretched between them, but it wasn't empty. It carried the weight of unspoken thoughts, of questions neither wanted to ask but both felt. Aarav had spent so much time running toward his ambitions that he had never stopped to consider what he might be leaving behind.

"You don't have to choose, you know," Aisha finally said. "Not everything has to be either here or there. Sometimes, the in-between is where we truly find ourselves."

Aarav smiled faintly. "You make it sound so simple."

"It's not," she admitted. "But that doesn't mean it's impossible."

They sat in quiet companionship, the cool breeze carrying the scent of jasmine from the garden below. Aisha traced patterns on the stone floor with her fingers, her expression lost in thought. She had her own life, her own path, and yet, in this moment, she seemed as caught in uncertainty as he was.

"I envy you," she said suddenly.

Aarav raised an eyebrow. "Why?"

"Because you have the choice to leave, to explore. Not everyone does. Some of us have to stay and make peace with where we are."

Her words struck a chord. Aarav had always viewed his departure as an escape, but perhaps it was also a privilege. Aisha, for all her wisdom and clarity, was bound by ties he didn't fully understand. And yet, she carried it all with such grace.

As the night deepened, they shared stories—of childhood adventures, of lost friendships, of dreams they once had. It wasn't romance, not yet, but it was understanding. And in that understanding, Aarav found a moment of peace.

The next morning came too soon. The house bustled once more, this time with the preparations of departures. His mother fussed over his packed bags, slipping extra snacks into the pockets. His father stood by the doorway, his expression unreadable but his eyes carrying the depth of a thousand unspoken words.

"Take care of yourself, beta," his mother whispered, pressing a hand to his cheek.

Aarav nodded, his throat tightening. He turned to his father, who gave him a single pat on the back, firm and full of meaning. "You'll do well. Just don't forget where you come from."

Aisha stood at the gate, watching as Aarav stepped into the waiting car. Their eyes met for a fleeting moment, and she gave him a small, knowing smile. No promises, no expectations—just an unspoken understanding that life had a way of circling back when it was meant to.

As the car pulled away, Aarav looked back at the town that had built him, at the home that had shaped him. He wasn't sure what awaited him in the city, but for the first time, he wasn't running toward or away from anything.

He was simply moving forward.

16
The Weight of Expectations

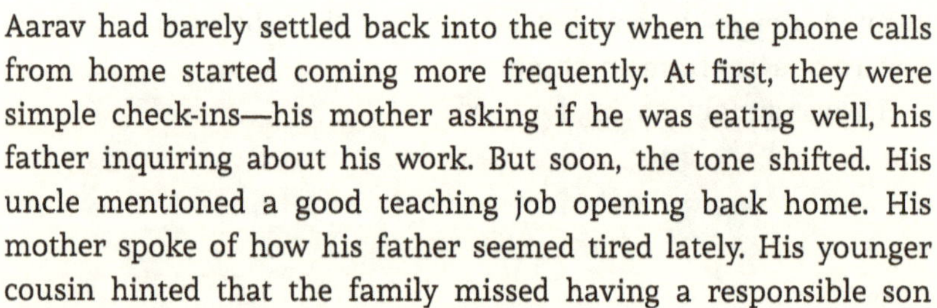

Aarav had barely settled back into the city when the phone calls from home started coming more frequently. At first, they were simple check-ins—his mother asking if he was eating well, his father inquiring about his work. But soon, the tone shifted. His uncle mentioned a good teaching job opening back home. His mother spoke of how his father seemed tired lately. His younger cousin hinted that the family missed having a responsible son around.

"Beta, your father has worked so hard for you," his mother said one evening. "He won't say it, but he needs you here. You have a good job now. Why do you still need to stay in that big city?"

Aarav sighed, gripping the phone. "Ma, I'm doing this for us, for my future."

"But what about our future?" she asked softly. "Aren't we a part of it?"

The weight of her words settled in his chest long after the call ended. He sat alone in his small apartment, staring at the blinking city lights outside his window. Was he being selfish? Had he truly left his family behind for his own dreams, without thinking of what they needed?

Aisha had noticed the shift in him. They had grown closer since the wedding, spending long evenings talking about everything from childhood memories to their fears about the future. But lately, she could see the worry in his eyes.

Aisha had always belonged to the small town where Aarav grew up, her presence woven into the fabric of his childhood. But unlike him, she had left much earlier, her family moving to the city when she was still in school. While Aarav had always seen the city as an intimidating maze of ambition and unfamiliar faces, for Aisha, it had slowly become home. The transition hadn't been easy—she had struggled to find her place, to blend into a world that moved too fast, spoke too loud, and often felt too distant. But over the years, she had learned to adapt, to carve out a space for herself in its restless rhythm. And now, as fate would have it, the city that had once separated them was the same place that had brought them back together.

"You're not really here, Aarav," she said one evening as they sat on a park bench. "Your mind is somewhere else."

He exhaled. "It's my family. They want me to come back. And maybe... maybe they're right."

Aisha studied him for a moment before speaking. "You love them, I know that. But is going back what *you* want? Or is it just guilt?"

He had no answer.

The pressure only grew stronger. His father, once silent, finally spoke up during a family call. "Aarav, this city life is not for us. You have done enough. Come back home."

For the first time, Aarav felt his father's disappointment, not in words but in the silence that followed. It was a quiet, unspoken plea.

The city had once been his escape, but now, it felt like a battleground. He was torn between two lives—one he had built with ambition and another tied to his roots. And then there was Aisha.

She had become a part of his world, but she had made it clear: she believed in dreams, in chasing something bigger.

"If you go back," she said, "do you think you'll be happy?"

He didn't know anymore. And that terrified him.

The following weeks were filled with endless contemplation. Aarav found himself wandering the city late at night, revisiting places that once gave him comfort—his favorite coffee shop, the park where he found solace after long days, the small bookstore where he had dreamed of buying his first novel. But the charm had faded. Every street, every building, now carried a question: *Is this really where I belong?*

At work, he found himself distracted. His boss noticed. "Something's off with you, Aarav. You're usually focused, driven. What's going on?"

He forced a smile. "Just... personal stuff."

But the truth was, his mind was miles away, in a home where his father sat silently at the dinner table, where his mother prepared meals with one less plate on the counter. He imagined his younger cousins asking when he'd visit next, his uncle shaking his head at the idea of Aarav choosing ambition over duty.

One evening, Aisha invited him to a rooftop gathering with friends. He went, but his heart wasn't in it. As laughter echoed around him, he realized he felt like a guest in his own life.

Aisha pulled him aside. "You're drifting, Aarav. If you're going to make a choice, make one. Don't let it be made for you."

He looked at her, really looked at her—the girl who challenged him, who understood his conflict, who might be the only person in this city who truly saw him.

"And if I leave?" he asked quietly.

She hesitated. "Then I hope it's because you *want* to, not because you feel you have to."

Her words stuck with him. He knew a decision was coming. And no matter what he chose, something—or someone—would be left behind.

Aarav spent the next few nights in restless sleep, his dreams a tangled mix of home and city life. He dreamt of his father standing by the fields, calling his name. He saw his mother waiting by the door, looking down the road as if expecting him to return. And then there was Aisha, fading into the distance as he walked away.

He woke up one morning with a sudden urgency, a weight heavier than before. His phone buzzed—another missed call from home. The walls of his apartment, once a place of comfort, now felt stifling.

It was time to decide.

But how do you choose between the life that made you and the one you built for yourself?

17
The Breaking Point

Aarav had spent weeks caught between two worlds, but life had a way of making choices for those too afraid to make them themselves. The call came late one night. He had just returned from work, exhaustion settling deep in his bones, when his phone buzzed violently on the table. It was his mother.

His fingers trembled as he answered. "Ma?"

Her voice was unsteady. "Beta... your father... He collapsed."

The words stole the breath from his lungs. "What? How? Is he—?"

"He's in the hospital. The doctors are saying it's exhaustion, stress... They want to keep him under observation. Aarav, come home. We need you."

The urgency in her voice shattered something within him. He had always thought of his father as unbreakable—a man who carried burdens without complaint. And now, he was lying in a hospital bed because of those very burdens.

Aarav packed without thinking. Clothes thrown haphazardly into a suitcase, his mind running through every scenario. By the time he reached the train station, his phone vibrated again. Aisha.

"Aarav, what's going on? You left without saying anything."

His throat was dry. "My father's in the hospital. I have to go."

There was silence on the other end before she spoke. "Do you know when you'll be back?"

"No."

Another pause. "Aarav... are you coming back at all?"

He had no answer.

The journey home felt longer than ever. Every passing field, every familiar station brought him closer to a life he had tried so hard to balance. As the train rattled through the night, he couldn't help but reflect on the crossroads before him. He had worked so hard to carve out an independent life, to prove that he could exist outside the shadow of his family's expectations. And yet, at that moment, nothing mattered more than getting home.

When he finally stepped off the train, the sight of his younger cousin waiting for him sent a fresh wave of anxiety through his chest.

"Bhaiya!" His cousin rushed forward, taking Aarav's bag. "Chacha is stable now, but... he keeps asking for you."

Aarav nodded, his footsteps hurried. The hospital smelled of antiseptic and worry. When he entered the room, his mother was seated by the bedside, holding his father's hand.

His father looked smaller than Aarav remembered. The lines on his face were deeper, his once-strong hands resting weakly on the white sheets. When he saw Aarav, a tired smile flickered across his face. "You came."

Aarav swallowed hard. "Of course I did."

His father gestured for him to sit. "Son... this family is not just mine to carry. It's yours too. I won't force you, but we need you."

His mother squeezed Aarav's shoulder. "Beta, we won't tell you what to do. But think about it. This is your home. Your roots. Your family."

Aarav sat there for hours, torn between duty and the life he had built. But something had changed. His father's weakened state had made one thing clear—life was unpredictable, and every choice came with a cost.

The next morning, Aisha's name flashed on his screen. He let it ring for a long moment before finally answering.

"Aarav," she exhaled. "Are you okay?"

"I don't know."

"What are you going to do?"

Aarav looked around—the house, the fields, the town that had shaped him. He knew the answer was no longer just about him.

"I think... I think I have to stay."

Aisha didn't respond right away. When she did, her voice was softer than he had ever heard it. "I had a feeling you'd say that."

"I never wanted it to end like this," he admitted. "I just... I can't leave them now."

"I understand, Aarav. And I won't ask you to choose me over them." There was a pause before she added, "But it doesn't mean this doesn't hurt."

He felt a lump rise in his throat. "Aisha—"

"No, it's okay. You're doing what's right. And I respect that. Just... promise me one thing?"

"Anything."

"Don't lose yourself in this. Whatever happens, don't forget the dreams you had before all this happened. You owe that to yourself."

Aarav closed his eyes, gripping the phone tighter. "I'll try."

"Goodbye, Aarav."

The line went dead.

That evening, he sat outside, staring at the fields that stretched endlessly before him. The house behind him was alive with murmurs of relatives, worried whispers, and hushed conversations about his father's recovery. And yet, all he could hear was Aisha's voice in his head.

Don't lose yourself in this.

He had made his decision, but the weight of it was heavier than he had ever imagined.

The next few days passed in a blur. Aarav found himself slipping into old routines—helping with household chores, listening to neighbors talk about their concerns, sitting beside his father as he slowly regained his strength. Each day felt like a reminder of the life he had left behind, and the life that was pulling him back.

His mother noticed his silence. "Beta, you've always carried too much on your shoulders. I see it in your eyes."

He forced a smile. "I'll be okay, Ma."

But would he? The weight of expectation, the suffocating familiarity of home, the love and duty that bound him—it was all-consuming. A part of him longed to be free, but another part knew that freedom came at a cost.

One evening, his father called him outside. The sun was setting, casting long shadows over the fields. "Aarav," he said softly, "I know you have dreams beyond this place. And I know you stayed because of me."

Aarav shook his head. "It's not just about you, Baba. It's about all of us."

His father nodded. "That's what I was afraid of. That one day, you would give up what you wanted for what we needed."

Aarav looked away, his chest tightening. "What if I don't have a choice?"

His father placed a hand on his shoulder. "There's always a choice, beta. Just make sure you're choosing for yourself, not just for us."

Aarav stayed silent, staring at the fading light. He had already made his choice. But the question lingered—had he made it for himself, or for the weight of everything he had been taught to carry?

18

Echoes of Yesterday

The night was eerily quiet, save for the rhythmic hum of the ceiling fan. Aarav lay on his bed, eyes fixed on the dim glow of the streetlight filtering through the curtains. His heart felt heavier than it had in years. The weight of his decision, of leaving behind everything he had known, was beginning to settle in, creeping through his chest like a slow, relentless tide. He was no stranger to sacrifice, but this—this felt different. This wasn't just about his family, his hometown, or even his future. This was about her.

It had been months since he last saw her, but her presence lingered in his mind like an old song stuck on repeat. He closed his eyes, allowing the memories to wash over him.

He could still remember the first time he met her in person. The nervous energy, the awkward laughter, the way she had tucked a stray strand of hair behind her ear while pretending not to notice how intently he was looking at her. He had spent so many nights before that moment imagining how it would feel to finally be next to her, to hear her voice without the barrier of a phone screen. And yet, nothing could have prepared him for the real thing.

There was something about the way she spoke—fast, animated, always on the edge of a new thought—that made him feel like the world was spinning just a little too quickly, but he didn't mind. She was a force of nature, pulling him into her orbit, making him believe, even if just for a moment, that he belonged somewhere beyond the limits of his small town.

He remembered the stolen moments between their busy lives. The coffee shop where they'd sit for hours, her hands wrapped around a cup that she never actually drank from because she was too busy talking. The way she'd complain about the world, about people who didn't understand her, about the unfairness of everything. And yet, she always found a way to laugh at it all, as if to say, "What else can we do but keep going?"

He missed the way she would nudge him playfully when he got too serious, when he started overthinking, which, to be fair, was most of the time. "You think too much," she used to tell him. "Just let things be."

But he couldn't. He never could. And now, that very tendency had left him stranded in the space between past and future, between what was and what could have been.

Aarav turned on his side, pressing his fist against his chest, trying to will away the ache. He had been so focused on leaving, on proving himself, that he never stopped to think about what he was leaving behind. The late-night conversations, the fights that ended in laughter, the way she had understood him in ways he never thought possible. And now, she was just a memory—a ghost of a life he once had, slipping through his fingers no matter how tightly he tried to hold on.

He reached for his phone, his thumb hovering over her name in his contacts. He knew she had moved on. He had seen the pictures, heard the stories. But did she ever think about him the way he thought about her? Did she ever miss the little things? The way his voice sounded at 2 AM when he was too tired to filter his thoughts? The way he used to hold her hand absentmindedly, as if it was the most natural thing in the world? Did she ever stop, just for a second, and wonder what would have happened if things had been different?

A part of him wanted to call her, to hear her voice one last time, to tell her that she still haunted his dreams. But he knew better. Some things were meant to stay in the past. Some stories didn't get second chances.

But what if they did?

The thought sent a shiver through him. What if, just once, he allowed himself to break the rules he had built so rigidly? Would she pick up? Would she even recognize his voice, or had time blurred him into the background of her memories the way she remained vivid in his?

He hesitated, fingers trembling over the screen. A single call, a few words—would it change anything? Or would it only bring more pain? His mind wrestled between longing and reason, and for a fleeting moment, his heart whispered, "Take the risk."

Instead, he placed the phone back on the nightstand and turned away from it, as if that simple act could also turn away the longing in his heart. The echoes of yesterday would always be there, whispering to him in the quiet of the night, reminding him of what was lost.

And yet, morning would come. And with it, the reminder that life moves forward, even when the heart lingers in the past.

The sunlight would filter through the curtains, indifferent to the ache in his chest. The world would continue spinning, and he would have to keep moving with it. But for now, in the stillness of the night, he let himself feel the weight of what once was, of what would never be again. Because sometimes, memories were all we had left, and for a little while, they were enough.

19
The Weight of Expectation

The streets of his hometown felt different this time. Familiar yet distant, as if he were walking through a dream of his own past. Aarav had always thought that coming back would feel like a warm embrace, like stepping into a place where he truly belonged. But now, with every conversation, every glance exchanged with his family, he felt the weight of something unspoken pressing down on him.

His mother fussed over him more than usual, asking if he was eating properly, if he was sleeping well, if his job was treating him right. But her real questions lay in the pauses, in the way her voice softened when she asked, "How long will you stay this time?" There was something in her eyes—a quiet longing, a silent plea for him to stay longer, to not just be a guest in the home he grew up in.

His father, ever the quiet observer, didn't say much, but Aarav could sense the disappointment beneath his measured words. "The city life has changed you," he had remarked over dinner. It wasn't said with anger, just an undeniable truth. Aarav had felt it too. The boy who once dreamt under these skies, who found joy in the simplicity of his small town, was no longer the same. The world had called him away, and he had answered.

But the guilt gnawed at him. His parents were getting older. His father's hair had turned grayer, his mother's hands had grown rougher from years of hard work. They had sacrificed so much for him, and now, when they needed him the most, he was merely a visitor in their lives. He watched them move about their routine, their bodies slower than before, their laughter quieter, and he wondered—was his success worth the loneliness he had left behind for them?

The relatives didn't help either. "Your parents are alone most of the time," one aunt said, shaking her head. "You should think about settling down, being closer to them. What is all this success worth if you don't have your family beside you?" Another relative added, "You earn well, but money cannot replace the warmth of home."

Aarav wanted to argue, to explain that he wasn't abandoning them, that he was chasing a dream, that his ambitions were not a rejection of his roots but a testament to them. But the words felt hollow. He could see the longing in his mother's eyes, the quiet resignation in his father's silence, and he had no words that could take away their loneliness.

Late at night, he sat on the terrace of his home, staring at the stars that once held his wishes. They looked the same, but he felt different. He thought of her again. She had once told him that love was about being present, about showing up when it mattered. Was he failing at love—not just with her, but with his family too?

He remembered the nights he had spent with her on video calls, talking about dreams and futures, neither of them knowing where life would take them. She used to tell him, "One day, we'll figure it out." But they never did. And now, as he sat here, torn between two worlds, he realized how much he had let slip away.

His phone buzzed with messages from work. New projects, new opportunities—an entire future awaited him in the city. A future he had worked so hard to build. But at what cost?

The weight of expectation sat heavy on his chest. He was at a crossroads, torn between duty and desire, between past and future. And for the first time in his life, he wasn't sure which path to choose.

As the night stretched on, a quiet fear settled within him—what if, in chasing his dreams, he had lost the very people who had given him the courage to dream in the first place? And what if, in searching for his place in the world, he had left behind the one place where he truly belonged?

The past and the present collided in his mind. The laughter of his childhood echoed in the walls of his home, the memories of stolen moments with her lingered like whispers in the night. He thought of the festivals they had celebrated together, the old, carefree days when the world felt smaller and the heart felt fuller. He thought of the first time he had held her hand, the way she had smiled at him under the dim glow of streetlights, how she had understood him without words.

He leaned back against the chair, the cool breeze ruffling his hair, his heart heavy with emotions he could no longer ignore. The stars blinked down at him as if they, too, were waiting for him to decide.

Would he choose to stay, or would he continue chasing a life that kept pulling him further and further away?

20

A Heart Divided

The sun was just beginning to rise, casting a golden glow over the quiet town. Aarav sat by his bedroom window, staring out at the familiar streets, his mind a tangled web of emotions. He could hear the distant call of a vegetable vendor and the soft chatter of neighbors starting their day. This was home, the place where he had spent his childhood, where every street held a memory, and yet, it felt more distant than ever. The nostalgia was overwhelming, but so was the realization that he had become an outsider in his own home.

His mother had already begun her morning rituals—boiling tea, lighting a small diya in the prayer room, humming a hymn he had heard all his life. It was comforting, yet unsettling. He had spent so many years waking up to the sound of city traffic, rushed mornings, and endless notifications on his phone. Here, life moved slower, more deliberately. But was that a good thing? Or had he simply outgrown it?

His phone buzzed, jolting him out of his thoughts. A message from his boss reminding him about an upcoming meeting. Another from a colleague asking for his opinion on a report. The demands of his corporate life in the city were ever-present, calling him back to the world he had built with such determination. Yet, the weight of his family's expectations was pressing on him like never before.

At breakfast, his mother placed a plate of parathas in front of him, watching him with a gentle smile. "You used to eat four of these when you were younger. Now you barely finish two."

Aarav smiled weakly. "I guess my appetite has changed."

His father, seated at the other end of the table, cleared his throat. "Appetite isn't the only thing that changes. Priorities do too."

There it was—the conversation he had been dreading. His father had never been one for long discussions, but when he spoke, his words carried weight. Aarav put down his cup of tea and sighed. "I know what you're thinking, Papa."

His father looked at him, eyes filled with both pride and sadness. "Then you also know what I want to ask. How long do you plan to keep running between two lives?"

The question struck him harder than he expected. He had thought about it himself—countless times. The truth was, he didn't have an answer. He wanted both worlds, but could he have them?

"It's not that simple," Aarav finally said. "I worked hard for what I have. I can't just walk away."

His mother reached for his hand, her fingers warm and steady. "Beta, we don't want you to leave behind what you've built. We just don't want to be left behind either."

Her words settled deep in his chest. He looked at her, at the worry lining her face, the silent plea in her eyes. Was he being selfish? Was his success really worth the loneliness his parents felt in his absence? He had spent years chasing his dreams, believing that making something of himself would bring pride to his family. But had he considered what they truly wanted?

Later that day, he took a walk through the town, hoping fresh air would clear his mind. He passed by the old bookstore where he used to spend hours, the tea stall where he and his childhood friends had debated over the smallest things, the cricket field where he had spent

endless evenings. Every corner held a piece of him, a version of himself that still lingered in these streets. The memories were almost suffocating, reminding him of a simpler time when choices weren't so complicated.

Then, almost as if fate wanted to remind him of what he had left behind, he saw her.

She was standing by the lake, looking out at the water, lost in thought. His heart clenched at the sight of her—her presence like a familiar melody he had forgotten but still knew by heart. He hesitated, then took a step forward.

"Didn't think I'd see you here," he said, his voice softer than he intended.

She turned, her eyes widening for a moment before settling into something unreadable. "Aarav. You're back."

He nodded. "For a while."

She gave a small smile, but there was a distance in her gaze, a space time had carved between them. "It's been a long time."

"Yeah... it has."

The silence stretched between them, filled with words left unsaid. He wanted to ask her how she had been, if she had thought about him as much as he had thought about her. If she had missed the small, insignificant moments—the way he used to fix her coffee just right, the way their hands would brush while walking, the way she'd laugh at his worst jokes. But the past had already settled between them, immovable, unchangeable.

She sighed, looking back at the water. "You know, I used to think we would figure it all out. That somehow, things would just work themselves out. But life... it doesn't wait for anyone."

Aarav swallowed the lump in his throat. "I know."

She turned back to him, her eyes searching his. "Do you? Because you still seem like you're standing at the same crossroad."

Her words stung because they were true. He was stuck, caught between the past and the future, between home and ambition, between love and responsibility. And for the first time, he wondered—was there even a right choice?

As the sun dipped lower in the sky, Aarav realized something: no matter which path he chose, something would be left behind. The real question was—what was he willing to lose? And for the first time, he wasn't sure if he was ready to make that decision.

21
Shadows of the Past

The sky had turned a deep shade of orange as the sun dipped below the horizon, casting long shadows across the familiar streets of Aarav's hometown. He walked aimlessly, his feet moving on their own, drawn by an invisible pull of nostalgia. The scent of freshly baked sweets from the halwai's shop filled the air, mingling with the distant chime of the temple bell. Everything seemed unchanged, yet it all felt so different, as if time had preserved the setting but stolen the innocence of the boy who once roamed these streets.

He passed by his old school, where the rusted gates still stood tall, the peeling paint on the walls untouched by years of wear. The playground, where he had spent countless afternoons playing cricket, stretched out before him, silent and empty. He could almost hear the echo of his friends' laughter, feel the weight of the bat in his hands, relive the thrill of hitting a six. Life had been simple then—school, home, stolen moments of freedom, and dreams that had yet to be tested by reality.

His phone buzzed in his pocket, jolting him back to the present. It was a message from his boss, a reminder about an upcoming presentation that demanded his attention. Aarav sighed, the weight of his responsibilities pressing down on him like an unseen force. No matter how far he traveled, he was always tethered to the life he had built in the city.

And yet, here, in the town that had shaped him, he felt like a stranger.

Could a person truly belong to two worlds at once? Or was he merely clinging to a past he was too afraid to let go of?

His steps carried him to the lake—the very place where he had seen her earlier that day. He shouldn't have come back, shouldn't have reopened wounds that had barely healed, but something about this place called to him. The water shimmered under the moonlight, reflecting his own turmoil back at him.

Aarav sat on a bench near the shore, absently tracing patterns in the dust with his shoe. His mind was a whirlwind of emotions, tangled with questions he couldn't answer. And then, as if fate had orchestrated it, he heard soft footsteps behind him.

He turned, and there she was. Meera.

She stood a few feet away, hesitant, as if caught between approaching him and walking away. The moonlight illuminated her face, making her look just as she had years ago—young, hopeful, untouched by the burdens of time. But her eyes told a different story. They carried the weight of unsaid words, of choices made and paths abandoned.

"I thought you might be here," she finally said, her voice quiet but certain.

Aarav gave a small smile, gesturing to the empty space beside him. "Some places never change."

She hesitated before sitting down, keeping a careful distance between them. They both stared at the water, the silence stretching between them like an invisible thread, fragile yet unbroken.

"You left without saying goodbye," she murmured after a while.

Aarav sighed. "I thought it would be easier that way."

"Was it?" she asked, turning to look at him.

He met her gaze, seeing the echoes of their past in her eyes. "No."

She gave a sad smile, shaking her head. "I used to be so angry with you. I kept wondering what I did wrong, why you chose to walk away. But with time, I realized...it wasn't just me, was it?"

Aarav exhaled, running a hand through his hair. "No, it wasn't. I was afraid, Meera. Afraid of losing myself, of disappointing my family, of choosing wrong and regretting it forever. So I did the only thing that felt safe—I ran."

Meera looked back at the water, her fingers grazing the wooden bench. "And now? Do you still think running was the right choice?"

He was silent for a long moment, then shook his head. "I don't know. I thought I had everything figured out, but being back here...it's messing with me. It's making me question everything."

She smiled faintly. "That's the thing about home. It doesn't just remind you of who you were; it forces you to confront who you've become."

Aarav felt a lump form in his throat. He wanted to tell her how much he had missed her, how many times he had thought about reaching out but had stopped himself. But what good would it do now? The past was the past, and no amount of regret could rewrite it.

"I saw your father at the market today," Meera said suddenly, changing the subject. "He looked...older."

Aarav's chest tightened. He had noticed it too—the gray strands in his father's hair, the subtle stoop of his once-proud shoulders. "Yeah," he said quietly. "Time does that."

Meera studied him for a moment before speaking. "You know, he doesn't say it, but he misses you. They both do. They just don't know how to show it."

Aarav looked down at his hands. "I know."

"Then why are you still hesitating?"

He let out a humorless chuckle. "Because the moment I choose one life, I lose the other."

Meera placed a hand on his, warm and familiar. "Maybe it's not about choosing, Aarav. Maybe it's about finding a way to make both worlds coexist."

Her words lingered long after she had left, and as Aarav sat alone by the lake, he realized something profound.

Perhaps the hardest choices in life weren't about picking one path over another. Perhaps the real challenge was learning how to walk both roads without losing yourself along the way.

The wind whispered through the trees, carrying with it the echoes of the past and the uncertainty of the future. And for the first time in a long while, Aarav knew that no matter what lay ahead, he had to find his own way through it all.

22

Crossroads of the Heart

Aarav lay awake in his childhood room, staring at the ceiling as the echoes of his conversation with Meera refused to fade. The quiet hum of the ceiling fan filled the silence, yet his mind buzzed with a noise far louder. Every word, every lingering glance from the night before replayed like an old song he couldn't turn off.

Her words had cut through the carefully constructed walls he had built around himself. *Maybe it's not about choosing… maybe it's about making both worlds coexist.* But was that even possible? The city had shaped him into a man of ambition, while his hometown reminded him of the roots he had almost abandoned. Could he truly belong to both?

The next morning, as he sat with his parents at the breakfast table, he noticed the subtle changes in them—his mother's wrinkled hands moving slower than before, his father's once-firm voice now carrying a hint of fatigue. He had spent years convincing himself that they were fine without him, but seeing them now, he wasn't so sure.

"Beta, eat properly," his mother chided, placing another roti on his plate. "You've lost weight."

Aarav forced a smile. "Work keeps me busy, Ma."

His father, who had been silently reading the newspaper, finally spoke. "Busy is good. But too much of it, and you forget what really matters."

The words weren't spoken with anger, but they carried weight. Aarav looked up, their eyes meeting for a brief moment before his father turned back to the paper.

The room felt heavy with unspoken emotions. His father had always been a man of few words, but the disappointment in his gaze was clear. Aarav wanted to tell them everything—about his doubts, his struggle, the way he constantly felt torn between duty and desire. But the words refused to come.

Later that day, he found himself at the lake again, his sanctuary in times of turmoil. This time, it wasn't Meera who found him, but an old friend—Rohan.

"You look like a man carrying the weight of the world," Rohan said, dropping down onto the bench beside him.

Aarav let out a humorless chuckle. "Maybe I am."

Rohan stretched out his legs, tossing a small stone into the water. "Let me guess. Family wants you to stay, but your dreams are elsewhere?"

Aarav nodded. "Something like that."

"I get it, man. I stayed back, took over the family business. And some days, I wonder—what if I had left? Would I have been happier?"

Aarav turned to him. "And?"

Rohan sighed. "I don't have the answer. But I do know this—no matter where you go, you'll always miss the other life. The trick is figuring out which one you can't live without."

Aarav exhaled, staring at the rippling water. Rohan's words settled deep within him. He had always thought of his choices as an either-or situation, but maybe life wasn't that black and white.

As the day stretched on, Aarav made his way through the town, revisiting old places, talking to familiar faces. He found himself outside Meera's house, an invisible pull drawing him there. He hesitated before knocking.

She opened the door, surprise flickering across her face before she stepped aside, letting him in. The house smelled the same—jasmine and old books. It felt like stepping into a memory.

"I didn't think I'd see you again so soon," she said, offering him tea.

"I needed to talk," Aarav admitted.

Meera studied him, then nodded. "Alright."

They sat across from each other, the weight of their past sitting between them. Aarav took a deep breath. "Do you ever wonder what would've happened if things had been different?"

Meera smiled wistfully. "All the time. But we made our choices, Aarav."

He looked down at his cup. "And what if we had chosen wrong?"

She reached across the table, her fingers barely brushing his. "Then maybe we still have time to make it right."

Her words sent a shiver down his spine. Aarav had always believed that life moved forward, that once a door closed, it stayed shut. But for the first time in years, he wondered—was it possible to turn back, to fix what was broken, to find balance between the past and the future?

As he stepped out of Meera's house, the weight on his chest felt just a little lighter. He didn't have all the answers, but he knew one thing for certain—his time in this town wasn't over yet. And maybe, just maybe, neither was their story.

That night, he walked the quiet streets alone, feeling something he hadn't felt in years—a sense of belonging. Not just to the past, not just to the future, but to this moment, where both met in a delicate balance. He wasn't running anymore. He was standing still, finally ready to face what came next

23
The Weight of Choices

The days in his hometown stretched longer than Aarav had expected. Time, which once seemed to race against him in the city, now moved at a pace that forced him to reflect. His mornings were spent helping his mother in the kitchen, afternoons listening to his father's stories—some he had heard countless times before, others revealing parts of the man he had never known. Evenings were his own, filled with solitary walks around the lake or quiet conversations with Meera.

He had convinced himself that this visit was temporary, a necessary pause before he returned to the life he had built. But with each passing day, that conviction wavered.

One evening, as he walked past the familiar lanes of his childhood, he was greeted by an unexpected sight—his younger cousin, Anuj, pacing outside his home with a nervous energy Aarav immediately recognized.

"What's wrong?" Aarav asked, falling into step beside him.

Anuj exhaled sharply. "It's Ma and Papa. They're setting up my engagement. I don't even know the girl properly, and they expect me to just agree."

Aarav studied the frustration on Anuj's face. He saw a reflection of his own younger self—the same quiet rebellion, the same struggle between love for family and personal dreams. He thought back to his own battles, the nights he had spent questioning his choices.

"What do you want?" Aarav finally asked.

Anuj scoffed. "Does it matter? In the end, we do what they want."

Aarav was silent for a moment. Then, softly, he said, "It does matter. If you don't fight for what you want now, you'll always wonder what could have been."

Anuj looked at him, searching for something in his expression. "And what about you, bhaiya? Are you fighting for what you want?"

Aarav opened his mouth to respond, but the words refused to come. Was he? Or was he simply waiting for life to decide for him?

Later that night, he found himself outside Meera's house again. This time, she was waiting for him, a knowing smile on her lips.

"You're thinking too much again," she said, handing him a cup of chai.

Aarav chuckled. "Maybe."

They sat on the veranda, the cool breeze carrying the scent of wet earth. He took a sip of the tea, savoring its warmth.

"Meera," he began hesitantly, "do you ever regret the choices you made?"

She looked at him, her gaze unwavering. "Regret? No. But sometimes, I do wonder what life would've been like if I had chosen differently."

Aarav nodded, his thoughts mirroring hers. "Do you think we can ever really have both? The life we dream of and the life we owe to our family?"

Meera's smile was tinged with sadness. "Maybe. But it takes courage to create that balance. The question is—do you have that courage, Aarav?"

He didn't answer. Not because he didn't know, but because, for the first time in a long time, he realized he had never truly asked himself that question.

As the night deepened, Aarav sat in silence, staring at the stars scattered across the sky. Choices, responsibilities, dreams—everything he had been running from now stood before him, demanding an answer.

And for the first time, he wasn't sure which path he would take.

24
The Weight of Unfinished Stories

Aarav walked through the narrow streets of his hometown, the familiar scent of rain-soaked earth mingling with the distant aroma of freshly brewed chai from the corner tea stall. The sun had begun to set, casting an amber glow over the town, making everything look like a faded photograph from his childhood. It was strange how everything had changed yet remained the same. The roads were still lined with small shops, the temple bells still rang at dusk, and the same laughter of children playing in the alleyways filled the air. But within him, a storm raged, a battle between the past and the future, between duty and desire.

His conversation with Meera replayed in his mind. *Then maybe we still have time to make it right.* The words had lingered long after he left her house, sinking deep into his thoughts. Was it possible to mend what had been broken? Or was he clinging to a past that no longer existed?

That night, as he sat at the dining table with his parents, he couldn't help but notice the small things—the way his mother still served food before sitting down to eat herself, the way his father's hands trembled slightly as he held his glass of water. These were details he had overlooked for years, lost in the rush of city life.

"Beta, you've been quiet today," his mother observed, breaking the silence.

Aarav forced a smile. "Just thinking."

His father put down his spoon and looked at him carefully. "Thinking about what?"

Aarav hesitated. Should he tell them? Should he share the weight he had been carrying for so long?

"About choices," he finally said, his voice quieter than he intended.

His father nodded knowingly. "Life is full of them. Some easy, some impossible."

His mother sighed. "Sometimes we think we have a choice, but in the end, the heart decides for us."

Aarav wanted to argue, to say that he had been making logical choices all his life, but deep down, he knew his mother was right. Hadn't his heart already made its decision? He just hadn't been willing to accept it.

Later that night, he found himself scrolling through old messages on his phone—conversations with Meera from years ago. There was a time when they had talked about everything, when the future felt like something they would shape together. But somewhere along the way, life had pulled them in different directions, leaving them stranded on opposite shores.

His thoughts were interrupted by a call from Rohan. "Meet me at the lake," his friend said, his voice urgent.

When Aarav arrived, he found Rohan sitting on the bench, staring at the still water. "What's wrong?" Aarav asked, sitting beside him.

Rohan exhaled slowly. "I proposed to Aditi today."

Aarav's eyes widened. "That's great news! Why do you look like someone just punched you in the gut?"

Rohan let out a humorless chuckle. "Because she said she needs time to think."

Aarav frowned. "Why? I thought things were good between you two."

"They are," Rohan admitted. "But she's afraid of the future. She has dreams, ambitions. She thinks staying here with me will mean giving them up."

Aarav felt a pang of recognition. It was the same dilemma he faced, just in reverse.

Rohan turned to him. "You always said city life gave you purpose, but did it ever give you peace?"

Aarav didn't have an answer. Instead, he stared at the reflection of the moon in the lake, distorted by the ripples. Maybe life was never meant to be clear, never meant to be easy. Maybe it was about finding clarity within the chaos.

The next morning, he met Meera again, this time at the old bookstore they used to visit as teenagers. The place was almost unchanged—dusty shelves filled with forgotten stories, the faint scent of old paper and ink lingering in the air.

Meera ran her fingers along the spines of books. "Do you remember how we used to hide our favorite books here, hoping no one would buy them?"

Aarav chuckled. "Yeah. I think my copy of *The Alchemist* is still behind that shelf."

She smiled but then turned serious. "Have you made a decision, Aarav?"

He looked at her, really looked at her. The girl he had once loved was now a woman who had lived, who had faced her own battles. And yet, when he was with her, it felt like no time had passed at all.

"I don't know if I ever truly left," he admitted. "Maybe I was just running, thinking I could escape the pull of home, of you. But I can't."

Meera's eyes softened. "Then maybe it's time to stop running."

For the first time in years, Aarav felt something shift inside him. The past wasn't just a memory; it was a part of him. And maybe, just maybe, it was time to embrace it.

That evening, he took a long walk through the town, stopping at places that once meant something to him—his school, the abandoned cricket ground, the little café where he and Meera used to sit for hours. Each step brought back memories, a past he had once tried to escape but now found himself longing to reclaim.

As he reached the lake once again, he saw Meera waiting for him, her silhouette framed against the setting sun. He took a deep breath and walked toward her, realizing that for the first time in a long time, he wasn't torn between two worlds. He was exactly where he needed to be.

25

The Crossroads of the Heart

The morning sun streamed through the gaps in the curtains, casting warm golden streaks across Aarav's room. He had barely slept. His mind had been a battlefield of memories, decisions, and emotions that refused to settle. The words Meera had said the night before echoed in his thoughts. *Then maybe it's time to stop running.* Was he ready to accept that? Was he truly ready to redefine his life?

Downstairs, the clatter of utensils and the faint aroma of ginger tea pulled him from his restless thoughts. He made his way to the kitchen, where his mother was busy preparing breakfast. She turned and smiled as she saw him standing by the door.

"You're up early," she remarked, setting down a plate of freshly made parathas.

Aarav sat down at the table and took a deep breath. "Ma... have you ever regretted a decision?"

His mother paused for a moment, then sat across from him. "Life is full of decisions, beta. Some feel right in the moment but hurt later. Some feel wrong initially but turn out to be blessings."

He nodded slowly, contemplating her words. "What if you're caught between two choices—one that honors your responsibilities and another that honors your heart?"

She looked at him thoughtfully. "Then you must ask yourself—what would make you truly happy? Not in the short term, but in the years to come."

Aarav stared at his plate, appetite lost. He had spent years building a life in the city, chasing dreams that had once seemed so essential. But now, the life he had left behind, the relationships he had abandoned, all pulled at him with a force stronger than he had ever imagined.

That afternoon, he walked through the town again, this time with clearer eyes. He noticed the small details he had once taken for granted—the way the tailor on the corner still hummed while he stitched, the way the old bookstore smelled exactly the same, the way the air carried the distant laughter of children playing cricket in the empty lot. He smiled, realizing how these seemingly small things were, in fact, the anchors of his childhood.

His thoughts drifted back to Meera. How many moments had he let slip through his fingers? How many times had he chosen ambition over love, thinking he had all the time in the world? The bookstore where they had met the previous evening still stood in its nostalgic silence. On impulse, he stepped inside, his fingers grazing the spines of old books, as if searching for a piece of the past that had been left behind.

A familiar voice interrupted his thoughts. "Did you find your copy of *The Alchemist*?"

He turned to see Meera standing there, arms crossed, a soft smile playing on her lips.

Aarav chuckled. "Turns out, some things don't stay hidden forever."

She studied him carefully. "And some things do."

He sighed, running a hand through his hair. "Meera, if I stay... will it change anything?"

She hesitated before responding. "Maybe. Maybe not. But at least you won't be running anymore."

Her words lingered between them, heavy with meaning. For the first time, Aarav allowed himself to imagine a life where he wasn't just chasing success but nurturing relationships that made life worth living. He thought of the endless nights he had spent in his high-rise apartment, staring out at a city that never truly felt like home. He had believed that success was the answer to every question, but standing there in the bookstore, he realized it had only been a distraction from the questions that mattered most.

The memories of their time together flooded his mind—the way she used to tilt her head slightly when she laughed, the way her eyes sparkled when she spoke about books, the way she always found beauty in the simplest of things. He remembered the long conversations under the dim streetlights, the silent walks along the riverbank, the unspoken promises in shared glances. Love had never been grand declarations or dramatic gestures; it had always been hidden in the quiet moments, in the small details he had only come to cherish after they were gone.

That night, as he lay in bed staring at the ceiling, he knew the time for hesitation was over. The past, the present, and the future were colliding in front of him, demanding a decision. And for the first time in years, he was ready to choose—not just for duty, not just for ambition, but for himself.

The next day, he would take his first step towards an answer. But for now, he let himself feel the weight of everything—the love he had lost, the dreams he had chased, and the possibility of something new waiting just beyond the horizon. His heart, long burdened with the expectations of others, finally began to whisper what it had wanted all along.

And this time, he was ready to listen.

26
The First Step

The morning air was crisp, carrying with it the faint scent of wet earth and the distant hum of life beginning anew. Aarav stood by the balcony of his old room, staring out at the town that had once been his entire world. The rooftops, the narrow lanes, the sleepy morning chaos—it all felt familiar yet foreign, like an old song whose lyrics he had forgotten but still hummed instinctively.

For the first time in years, he wasn't waking up to the sound of traffic, deadlines, or the urgency of an alarm clock. He was waking up to something far more unsettling—his own thoughts.

Downstairs, his father sat in his usual chair, reading the newspaper, the creases on his forehead more pronounced than Aarav remembered. His mother moved around the kitchen, her bangles clinking as she worked, her presence both comforting and distant.

As Aarav walked in, his father barely glanced up. "So, have you decided?"

It wasn't a question. It was a challenge. A reminder that no matter how long he had stayed away, some battles would always be waiting for him at home.

"I don't know yet," Aarav admitted, pouring himself a cup of chai.

His father sighed, folding the newspaper. "A man must know, Aarav. Uncertainty is for those who have the luxury of time."

Aarav met his father's gaze. "And what if I don't want to choose between family and my own life? What if there's a middle ground?"

His father scoffed, shaking his head. "Middle grounds are illusions. You either stay, or you leave. That's how life works."

Aarav wanted to argue, but the truth was, he wasn't sure himself.

Later that evening, he found himself walking towards the bookstore again. He wasn't sure if he was going there for a book or for Meera, but either way, his steps led him straight to her.

She was leaning against a shelf, flipping through the pages of an old novel. When she saw him, she smiled but said nothing.

"I think I'm staying," Aarav finally said.

She raised an eyebrow. "Think?"

He exhaled sharply. "Okay. I *am* staying."

Meera closed the book and looked at him carefully. "And what happens next?"

"I don't know," he admitted. "But for once, I'm not afraid of not knowing."

She studied him for a moment, then nodded. "That's a start."

As the evening deepened and the streetlights flickered on, Aarav realized something—maybe life wasn't about choosing between two worlds. Maybe it was about learning how to build bridges between them.

And maybe, just maybe, he had finally taken his first step.

27
Between What Was and What Will Be

———◦♡◦———

The night had settled over the town, casting a quiet hush over the familiar streets. The small roadside stalls, once bustling with laughter and hurried conversations, now lay empty, their owners having retired to their modest homes. The distant hum of crickets filled the silence, a soft symphony that had once been a comforting backdrop to Aarav's childhood. The air carried the faint scent of rain, a reminder of the monsoons that once brought joy in the form of puddles and paper boats.

Aarav sat on the rooftop, the same one where he had spent countless evenings as a boy, gazing at the stars and weaving dreams far bigger than the town he had grown up in. But tonight, the vast sky above him didn't feel like a window to possibilities; it felt like a question. Was this where he truly belonged? Could he ever reconcile the past with the future and find a space where both could coexist?

His father's words from that morning still lingered in his mind. *"Middle grounds are illusions, Aarav. You cannot live with one foot in the past and the other in the future."* But Aarav refused to believe that. There had to be a way to exist in both worlds—to embrace his ambitions without severing the roots that held him together. He wasn't the same boy who had once run barefoot through these streets, but he wasn't a stranger either. He was something in between, and maybe that wasn't such a bad thing.

A gentle creak of the terrace door pulled him from his thoughts. Meera stepped out, wrapped in a shawl, her eyes scanning his face the way they always did—like she could read the emotions he didn't say aloud. She had always understood him, even in moments when he barely understood himself.

"Couldn't sleep?" she asked, settling down beside him.

He shook his head. "Too many thoughts."

She nodded knowingly and pulled her shawl tighter around herself. "Want to talk about it?"

Aarav sighed, his gaze locked on the horizon. "I feel like I'm standing on the edge of something. Like if I take one step forward, everything changes. And if I step back, I'll be stuck in the same place forever."

Meera was quiet for a long moment before she said, "Change is scary, but so is regret."

He turned to her, searching for an answer in her expression. "How did you do it? How did you leave everything behind and start fresh?"

Meera smiled softly, though there was a sadness in her eyes. "It wasn't easy. There were nights I missed home so much that it physically hurt. But I told myself that moving forward didn't mean erasing the past. It just meant carrying it differently."

Aarav let her words settle in his heart. He thought about his mother, the quiet way she accepted his long absences, her eyes lighting up every time he visited, as if she were seeing her son for the first time all over again. He thought about his father—his stern love, his quiet fears that Aarav would forget where he came from. He thought about his friends, the ones who had never left, who still found joy in the simple things. And then there was Meera—the one constant who had somehow woven herself into his life when he least expected it.

"Do you ever think about going back?" he asked softly.

She hesitated before answering. "Sometimes. But then I remind myself that home isn't just a place. It's the people who make you feel like you belong."

Aarav chuckled. "You always know what to say."

Meera nudged him playfully. "That's because you always need reminding."

They sat in silence, the kind that didn't need filling, watching as the town lay peacefully beneath them. The cool breeze carried the distant sound of a train whistle—someone else leaving, someone else returning. Life moving forward, even when people hesitated.

"Are you afraid?" Meera finally asked.

Aarav thought about it. "Yeah. But I think that's okay."

She smiled, a warmth in her eyes. "It is. Because fear means you're about to do something that matters."

He looked at her then, really looked at her—the girl who had walked into his life like a quiet storm, making him question everything he thought he knew. He didn't know what the future held, but in that moment, he wasn't afraid of not knowing.

Maybe that was enough.

Maybe that was the first step toward something new.

And maybe, just maybe, the journey ahead would be worth every uncertain step.

28
The Turning Point

The morning air was thick with the scent of damp earth, the aftermath of a night's unexpected rain. Aarav walked through the narrow streets of his hometown, his hands tucked deep into his pockets, his mind a storm of thoughts. Everything around him remained unchanged—familiar walls, known faces, the predictable rhythm of life—but something within him had shifted irreversibly.

He had always believed that coming home would bring clarity, that standing in the very place where his dreams first took root would remind him of who he was. But now, he only felt caught between two worlds—one that had shaped him and another that was calling him forward. It was as if the past and future were pulling him in opposite directions, and he was stranded in the middle, unable to move.

As he passed by the old tea stall, he noticed his father sitting there with some of the neighborhood elders, engaged in a quiet conversation. Aarav hesitated for a moment before stepping closer, hoping for a moment of connection. But as he listened, he realized they were discussing him.

"He's spent too long away," his father was saying, his voice laced with the quiet concern of a man trying not to show his fear. "The city changes people. I just don't want him to forget where he comes from."

One of the elders nodded, stirring his cup of tea thoughtfully. "But isn't that the point? We raise our children to go further than we did."

His father sighed, shaking his head. "I know. But sometimes, I wonder—what if going further means losing what matters most?"

Aarav felt a lump rise in his throat. He wanted to step in, to reassure his father that he hadn't forgotten, that he carried home within him no matter where he went. But would his words be enough? Would they ever be enough?

The sound of his phone vibrating in his pocket pulled him from his thoughts. He glanced at the screen—Meera. A small smile tugged at his lips as he answered.

"Hey," he said, his voice softer now.

"Hey," she replied, the warmth in her voice an immediate comfort. "I just wanted to check in. How's it going?"

Aarav exhaled slowly, kicking at a stray pebble on the road. "Confusing. I thought coming back would help me see things clearly, but it's only made things more complicated."

Meera was silent for a moment before she said, "That's how you know it's real."

"What do you mean?"

"If it were easy, it wouldn't mean as much," she explained. "You're at a crossroad, Aarav. You're trying to carry both your past and your future, and that's not a bad thing. It just means you have to decide which parts you'll hold onto and which ones you're willing to let go."

Her words settled in his mind like ripples on still water. He thought about his mother's quiet sacrifices, his father's unwavering beliefs, the love and expectation woven into every interaction. And then he thought about his dreams, the future he had fought for, the version of himself he had built piece by piece. Could both exist together? Or was he fooling himself?

"I just don't want to disappoint anyone," he admitted, his voice barely above a whisper.

Meera's voice was steady. "Aarav, at some point, you have to ask yourself—are you living for them, or are you living for yourself?"

He closed his eyes, letting her words sink in. Maybe this was the turning point, the moment where he would have to choose—not between his family and his ambitions, but between living in fear of regret or embracing the unknown.

And for the first time, he wasn't sure which scared him more.

That night, as he lay in bed staring at the ceiling, Aarav found himself revisiting the small moments—the laughter at the dinner table, the quiet nods of approval from his father, the long walks with Meera where words weren't always needed. Every piece of his life had led him here, to this moment of uncertainty, to this question that had no easy answer.

The weight of it pressed on his chest, but beneath that weight was something else—something he hadn't fully acknowledged before. Hope. The hope that maybe, just maybe, he could find a way to have both, to be both.

As the first light of dawn filtered through his window, Aarav took a deep breath. The road ahead was uncertain, but for the first time in a long time, he wasn't afraid of taking the step. Not for his father, not for Meera, but for himself.

29
The Burden of Choice

The morning sun spread its golden light over the small town, making everything look peaceful and familiar. Aarav walked through the narrow lanes, the same ones where he had once run barefoot as a child, laughing and chasing kites. But today, his steps felt heavy, as if he were dragging an invisible weight with him. The houses, the trees, the distant ringing of the temple bells—all of it carried memories, reminding him how much had changed. Some people had stayed, some had moved away, and now he found himself standing at the crossroads between those two paths.

In the courtyard, his father sat on the old charpai, sipping his morning tea. Aarav paused at the sight of him. His father looked older, his face lined with wrinkles that hadn't been there before, his posture not as straight as it once was. The man who had once carried Aarav on his shoulders now struggled with simple movements. His mother, inside the kitchen, was busy rolling out rotis, her hands moving with a rhythm that had remained unchanged for years. The familiar sound of the rolling pin striking the wooden slab filled the air, but today, it felt different. It was like a clock ticking down, marking the moments he had left with them under the same roof.

Aarav's chest tightened. He had always known, in an abstract way, that his parents had sacrificed so much for him, but now, it wasn't just a thought. It was something he could see in the lines on their faces, in the fading paint on the walls of their home, in the weariness in their movements. Every little thing in the house told a silent story of struggle, of choices made so he could have a better life. And now, he was faced with a decision that might break their hearts.

Needing air, he stepped outside and wandered through the town. As he walked, he began noticing things he had overlooked before.

An old man sat on his doorstep, staring at the road, his frail hands resting in his lap. Aarav recognized him—he had three sons, all living in different cities, building successful lives. Yet, here he was, alone, watching a road that rarely brought them back home.

At a tea stall, two middle-aged men sat talking. Aarav couldn't help but overhear their conversation.

"He only comes home for Diwali now," one of them said, shaking his head. "Parents dedicate their whole lives to their children, and in the end, they sit alone, waiting."

"That's just how things are now," the other man sighed. "Work, career, success first. Family later."

Aarav swallowed hard. He had heard conversations like this before, but today, it felt different. It felt personal. Was this where his future was heading? Would his father also sit outside one day, waiting for a son who rarely returned? Would his mother smile through the pain, cooking for two instead of three, forcing a cheerful voice on the phone whenever he said, "Next month, Ma. I'll come next month"?

His throat tightened, his eyes burned. He quickly wiped them. He wasn't weak. But if that was true, then why did it feel like he was about to make the biggest mistake of his life?

That night, as he lay in bed, sleep refused to come. He picked up his phone and stared at an unread message from Meera. She had always believed in him, always told him he was meant for bigger things. She was waiting for him to make a decision, to step forward without hesitation. But at what cost?

He had spent years chasing dreams, wanting to build something for himself, to prove that his parents' sacrifices had not been in vain.

But could he have both ambition and family? Or was he already too far down the path of leaving everything behind?

His gaze drifted to the window, where the moonlight cast long shadows on the walls of his small room. As a child, he had always thought this house was too small for his dreams. But tonight, he had never felt smaller.

The weight of his thoughts was unbearable. The sacrifices of his parents, the loneliness of the elders he had seen in the town, the stories of children who left and never fully returned—it all crushed him. He imagined his mother waiting for his calls, his father pretending not to miss him, their voices growing fainter with time.

He suddenly remembered something from his childhood. On cold winter nights, when the power went out, his parents would sit with him by the dim glow of an oil lamp, telling him stories. Back then, the world felt warm and safe, no matter how dark it was outside. Now, he realized, it wasn't the light of the lamp that had made him feel safe—it was them. And he was about to walk away from that warmth forever.

As exhaustion finally took over, one thought echoed louder than all the others: Was he chasing a future so fiercely that he was leaving behind the very people who had given him one?

30
The Weight of Goodbye

The morning after his sleepless night, Aarav sat on the terrace, watching the town wake up. The sun cast a golden glow over the rooftops, stretching long shadows across the quiet streets. The air carried the familiar scent of damp earth, mingling with the occasional waft of frying pakoras from a distant tea stall. These were the little details he had taken for granted, the small pieces of home that had always been there, unnoticed—until now. Every sound, every scent, every fleeting moment felt magnified, as if his mind was desperately trying to imprint these sensations before they became nothing more than distant memories.

He clutched his cup of chai, its warmth offering little comfort against the cold knot in his chest. His mind was tangled in a storm of emotions—duty, love, ambition, regret. He had spent so many years chasing dreams, running towards a future that now seemed uncertain. The thought of leaving his parents behind was unbearable, yet staying meant pushing aside everything he had worked for. The weight of the decision pressed down on him, suffocating and inescapable. It was as though he was standing at a crossroads, each path promising something different, but neither offering true peace.

His mother's voice broke his thoughts.

"Aarav, breakfast is ready," she called from below, her voice carrying the same warmth that had always made this house feel like home.

Slowly, he descended the stairs, finding his parents at the wooden dining table. The aroma of freshly made aloo parathas filled the air, but his appetite had long abandoned him. His father, unaware of the storm raging inside Aarav, read the newspaper, his eyes scanning the headlines with quiet focus. His mother placed a plate in front of him, her gentle smile filled with a love so unconditional, so pure, that it ached.

"You're lost in your thoughts these days," she said softly, brushing his hair back like she used to when he was a child.

He forced a smile. "Just work, Ma."

She didn't press further, but her eyes held an understanding he wasn't ready to face. He wanted to tell them. He wanted to pour his heart out, to confess that the thought of leaving them behind gnawed at his soul. That he was terrified of becoming another name in the long list of sons who visit once a year with gifts but leave behind empty chairs at dinner tables. That he had seen the loneliness in their future, and it shattered him.

Instead, he swallowed his words along with a bite of paratha, pretending everything was fine.

That afternoon, he wandered through the marketplace, letting the sights and sounds anchor him to the present. Shopkeepers shouted their prices, bargaining with customers over the cost of vegetables and spices. Children ran through the narrow lanes, laughing as they dodged carts and bicycles. The smell of freshly fried samosas drifted through the air, triggering a memory of him and Meera sharing a plate outside a college canteen. The way she used to steal the last bite just to tease him, the way her laughter felt like home—those moments had once seemed small, insignificant. Now, they felt like treasures he had carelessly let slip through his fingers.

Before he knew it, his feet had carried him to his old school. Its walls, though faded, remained unchanged, and the playground still echoed with the ghosts of his childhood. He traced his fingers over the rusted gate, feeling an odd sense of longing. It was here that he had dreamed of a life beyond this town, of a world filled with possibilities. But standing here now, all he could think of was how much he had left behind in pursuit of something bigger.

"Aarav?"

He turned to find Rohit, an old friend, now a man with tired eyes and a knowing smile. They sat on a bench nearby, reminiscing about the past until Rohit's voice took a somber tone.

"I moved back here last year. My parents needed me," he said. "You know, my father never said it, but I could see it in his eyes every time I left—how much it hurt. I thought I had all the time in the world to be with them. Until one day, I didn't."

Aarav felt the weight of those words settle in his chest. How many times had his father watched him leave, pretending it didn't hurt? How many nights had his mother sat in the quiet of their home, missing the sound of his voice? He had always thought they would be fine, that their love was strong enough to bridge any distance. But love, he realized, didn't erase loneliness. It merely softened its edges.

That night, he sat beside his father in the courtyard. The sky stretched above them, vast and indifferent to the turmoil in his heart. The chirping of crickets filled the silence, their song a constant hum in the background. The smell of damp earth lingered in the air, grounding him in the present even as his mind wandered to the past.

"Papa, do you ever regret not leaving this town for a bigger life?" Aarav asked hesitantly.

His father exhaled slowly, staring into the distance. "I had dreams, beta. Big ones. But then you were born, and suddenly, my dreams weren't about me anymore. They were about giving you the wings to fly."

A lump formed in Aarav's throat. "And what if I fly too far?"

His father smiled, but his eyes held a sadness Aarav had never noticed before. "That's the thing about being a parent. You want your child to soar, even if it means watching them disappear into the sky."

Aarav barely slept that night. His heart ached with the weight of a choice he wasn't sure he was ready to make. The image of his father's tired hands, of his mother's quiet understanding, replayed in his mind.

By morning, he knew one thing for certain—whatever decision he made, it would change everything.

And for the first time, he wasn't sure if he was ready for that change.

31
A Choice Beyond Time

The station was buzzing with life, yet Aarav stood still, feeling as if time had momentarily paused just for him. The rhythmic clatter of luggage wheels, the distant announcements blending with the sound of the train's whistle, the scent of freshly brewed chai from the vendors—it all felt too real and yet surreal at the same time. He was supposed to board the next train, to finally take the step he had been preparing for. Yet, his feet refused to move.

His parents stood beside him, their faces calm but their eyes betraying emotions they weren't saying out loud. His mother, as always, was fussing over his bag, making sure everything was in place, her hands trembling slightly as she zipped it shut. His father, a man of few words, simply adjusted his glasses and nodded, as if silently granting permission for his son to chase his dreams.

"You'll be fine," his mother said, trying to smile.

Aarav nodded. "You both will be, too."

But deep down, he wasn't sure.

As the train pulled into the station, his heartbeat quickened. This was it. The culmination of years of effort, of sacrifices, of choices that had led him here. Yet, in that moment, all he could think about was Meera.

He had thought he had moved on, had convinced himself that time would eventually dull the ache of what they once shared. But seeing her one last time before leaving had unraveled him. Her voice still echoed in his ears, soft yet laced with an edge of something unspoken.

"Aarav, you always said we were meant to meet. Maybe that was true. But maybe we were never meant to stay."

She had smiled then, the kind of smile that masked sorrow, that tried to pretend that everything was okay when it wasn't. He had stood there, wanting to say something, anything that would change what was already set in stone. But all he could do was watch her walk away, knowing that some distances could never be crossed, no matter how much the heart longed for it.

And now, standing here, he wondered—was he running toward his future, or was he running away from everything that truly mattered?

A final whistle rang through the air, jolting him from his thoughts. His father patted his shoulder, his mother wiped the corner of her eye discreetly, and he knew that if he hesitated any longer, they would tell him to stay. That he would crumble.

He took a deep breath, turned toward the train, and stepped forward.

But then he stopped.

He turned around, his heart hammering in his chest. His parents stared at him, surprised. His mother's lips parted slightly, as if she was about to say something but held back. His father's eyes, filled with quiet understanding, watched him closely.

Aarav took another step—**not toward the train, but toward them.**

"I can't do it," he whispered, more to himself than to them.

His father exhaled, relief flashing across his face before he composed himself. His mother reached for his hand, squeezing it tightly.

"Aarav... are you sure?" she asked softly.

He looked around, at the station filled with strangers chasing their own destinations, at the train that would have taken him miles away, at the past he had tried to leave behind and the future that now seemed uncertain. And then he looked at his parents—his home, his roots, the people who had given everything for him.

"I'm sure," he said, his voice steady. "Dreams change, Ma. And maybe mine wasn't what I thought it was."

Tears slipped down his mother's face as she pulled him into an embrace. His father placed a firm hand on his shoulder, nodding in silent approval. And in that moment, Aarav felt lighter than he had in years.

As they walked back home, under a sky painted in hues of orange and pink, Aarav realized something—**sometimes, the bravest choice isn't the one that takes you farthest, but the one that keeps you close to what truly matters.**

And for the first time in a long while, he knew he had made the right decision.

Aarav spent the following weeks rediscovering the place he had once wanted to escape from. He found himself lingering in the market, chatting with old vendors, watching the town move at its unhurried pace. He met with childhood friends who had stayed behind, who had built their lives here. And in their stories, he saw something he had never noticed before—a quiet contentment, a love for the life they had chosen.

He and Meera hadn't spoken since that day, but she was always there, lingering in his thoughts like an unfinished sentence. Then one evening, as he walked past the bookstore where they had spent countless hours browsing, he found her standing by the entrance, a book in her hands.

Their eyes met, and in that moment, everything else faded away.

"You didn't leave," she said, almost breathless.

"Neither did you," he replied.

A small smile tugged at her lips. "Maybe... we weren't meant to leave. Maybe we were meant to find our way back."

Aarav didn't know what the future held, but as he stood there with Meera, the setting sun casting a golden glow around them, he knew one thing—**home was never just a place. It was the people who made it worth staying for.**

And perhaps, just perhaps, he had found his way back to where he truly belonged.

Epilogue: The Roads We Choose

Years passed, but the moment Aarav stepped off that train platform remained etched in his heart. Life in the small town did not slow down, nor did it confine him. Instead, it expanded in ways he had never imagined. The choices he once feared making had led him to a life that felt more fulfilling than any distant dream ever could.

Aarav dedicated himself to building something meaningful—something beyond just a career, beyond expectations. He took over his father's small coaching center, transforming it into a thriving institute that helped young minds shape their futures. He mentored students who reminded him of his younger self, torn between duty and ambition. With each lesson he taught, he realized that knowledge was not just about escaping one's origins, but also about strengthening them.

His parents, now older, watched him with a quiet pride that words could never express. His father would sit outside the house every evening, sipping tea as he listened to Aarav talk about his students, about their struggles, their dreams. His mother, with her ever-watchful eyes, ensured that he never skipped a meal, that he still found moments to pause and appreciate life beyond work.

Yet, as Aarav sat beneath the old banyan tree, watching the golden hues of the evening sky, he couldn't ignore the things he had lost along the way. Aisha—her laughter, her unshaken belief in him, the quiet understanding they once shared—was now just a memory, a chapter closed yet never forgotten. Life had pulled them in different directions, and though he missed her, he chose to believe that wherever she was, she was happy. Perhaps that was the essence of life—some people walk with us for a while, shaping us in ways we don't realize until much later. And though their paths may diverge, the love, the lessons, and the moments remain, woven into the soul like an unspoken promise that everything happens as it should.

And then there was Meera.

They had found their way back to each other, though not in the way stories often romanticize. Their love had transformed into something deeper—something built on shared silences, knowing glances, and a history neither wished to rewrite. She had become a quiet but constant presence, someone who understood the weight of his choices without needing explanations. Their paths had diverged once, but in the end, life had brought them back to the same streets, the same sunsets, the same quiet understanding that some bonds never truly break.

One evening, as Aarav sat on the porch of his home, watching the sky turn to shades of orange and gold, Meera walked up beside him. She held out a book—one they had once spoken about but never got around to reading together. He smiled, taking it from her hands, their fingers brushing for just a second longer than necessary.

"Do you ever regret it?" she asked softly, not looking at him.

Aarav exhaled, his gaze fixed on the horizon. "No," he said. "Because I chose this life. And for the first time, I didn't just follow a path—I made my own."

She nodded, a knowing smile playing on her lips. The world around them moved at its unhurried pace, as it always had, as it always would. And in that stillness, Aarav knew—some dreams are not lost, they just change. And sometimes, the bravest thing we can do is stay.

As the sun dipped below the horizon, painting the world in the soft glow of twilight, Aarav turned to the woman beside him, to the home he had once thought he needed to leave, to the life he had built with his own hands.

And for the first time in a long while, he felt at peace.

The End.

www.ingramcontent.com/pod-product-compliance
Lightning Source LLC
Chambersburg PA
CBHW062228150726
47991CB00006B/2477